# "Those are my terms. Take it or leave it."

Shari shrugged with resignation and replied in a low, tormented voice, "Okay."

Grant walked toward her and lifted her chin. "What was that?" His gaze traveled over her face and searched her big brown eyes.

Shari looked up at him and Grant felt his blood rushing through his veins. "I said I will marry you."

"Then let's kiss on it." Before Grant knew what he was doing, he was lowering his head and slowly brushing his lips across Shari's. He hadn't meant to kiss her. He was still furious. He had intended to throttle her, but she looked so vulnerable, the way she had that night so many years ago, that again he was powerless to resist.

Her lips were soft and moist and she tasted as sweet as he remembered that night in the dorm. Grant lost himself in the kiss and circled his arm around her waist, pulling her closer to him. He deepened the kiss by using his tongue to trace the outline of her lips until she parted her mouth and opened up to him. He wrapped his tongue around hers, entwining it with his, sucking it, devouring it. Shari didn't object. She responded to his kiss.

The ringing of a cell phone snapped Grant out of the kiss just as if someone had poured cold water over him. What was he doing? He was kissing the woman who'd kept his son a secret from him for four years.

## Books by Yahrah St. John

Harlequin Kimani Romance

*Never Say Never*
*Risky Business of Love*
*Playing for Keeps*
*This Time for Real*
*If You So Desire*
*Two to Tango*
*Need You Now*
*Lost Without You*
*Formula for Passion*
*Delicious Destiny*

---

## YAHRAH ST. JOHN

is the author of ten books and numerous short stories. A graduate of Hyde Park Career Academy, she earned a bachelor of arts degree in English from Northwestern University. Her books have garnered four-star ratings from *RT Book Reviews,* Rawsistaz Reviewers, *Romance in Color* and numerous book clubs. In 2012, St. John was nominated for *RT Book Reviews* Reviewer's Choice Award for Best Series Romance. A member of Romance Writers of America, St. John is an avid reader of all genres. She enjoys the arts, cooking, traveling, basketball and adventure sports, but her true passion remains writing. St. John lives in sunny Orlando, the City Beautiful.

# Delicious
# Destiny

## YAHRAH ST. JOHN

HARLEQUIN® KIMANI™ ROMANCE

To my boyfriend, Freddie Blackman,
for all his love and support

Recycling programs
for this product may
not exist in your area.

ISBN-13: 978-0-373-86310-5

DELICIOUS DESTINY

Copyright © 2013 by Harlequin Books S.A.

**Printed in U.S.A.**

Dear Reader,

I hoped you enjoyed the conclusion to The Draysons: Sprinkled with Love trilogy. It was a pleasure to be included in the miniseries with wonderful writers such as A.C. Arthur and Farrah Rochon.

My goal was to use Shari Drayson's history with Dina and force a marriage of convenience with the love of her life—Grant. I heighten the drama with the You Take the Cake Competition as the backdrop. I thoroughly enjoyed researching baking, visiting Sweet Designs bakery in Orlando and watching a lot of *Cupcake Wars*.

Visit my website at www.yahrahstjohn.com for the latest updates or contact me via email at Yahrah@yahrahstjohn.com.

Warmest wishes,

Yahrah St. John

A huge thank-you to Susan and David Clippinger of Sweet Designs Kitchen in Hunter's Creek for showing me the bakery business. I couldn't continue to pursue my passion without my Dad, Austin Mitchell; 2nd moms, Asilee Mitchell and Beatrice Astwood; cousin Yahudiah Chodosh; sisters and BFFs Dimitra Astwood, Therolyn Rodgers, Tiffany Griffin and Tonya Mitchell, Kiara Ashanti and Bhushan Sukrham. You keep me grounded. To all my fans for their loyalty, you're simply the best.

# Prologue

"You have to come with me," Shari pleaded with her best friend and roommate, Dina English, as they sat in their dorm room at Ledgeman University. "Everyone from our graduate business class is going, and Grant is going to be there."

Shari had an enormous crush on Grant Robinson, the six-foot-tall graduate student who was the object of her fantasies. He was breathtakingly handsome and brilliant. He was the only student she knew who dressed up when he came to class, usually in trousers, a button-down shirt and loafers. The problem was that Grant could have any girl he wanted, so why was she pining for a man she could never have? Could it be because he was every bit as nice as he seemed? In class, he always treated Shari with respect, as if her ideas and opinions mattered.

"All right, I'll go." Dina sighed. "Otherwise, I'll never hear the end of it."

"You're a lifesaver." Shari breathed a sigh of relief. If Dina hadn't agreed, Shari wouldn't have felt confident enough to go by herself. At five foot nine, Dina was slim and gorgeous, with fair skin and high cheekbones. She was easily one of the most popular girls on campus. Meanwhile, Shari was five feet six inches with brown skin, a round face, large nose and a curvy figure.

Shari busied herself getting ready for the party that night, humming happily the whole time.

A few hours later, they arrived at the Omega Psi Phi's party. Dina wore skinny jeans and a flattering halter top and looked as if she had walked off the pages of *Essence.* The best Shari had been able to manage was black jeans and a print T-shirt. Since she'd been at Ledgeman, Shari had gained the infamous "freshman fifteen" and hadn't been able to take off the extra weight.

Dina worked the party, flirting with several men, leaving Shari to her own devices. Shari was nervous about seeing Grant, so she downed cup after cup of beer. The party became a blur. She did remember, however, the moment Grant stepped in, like a knight in shining armor, and told her he was taking her back to her dorm because she'd had too much to drink. To have the object of her affection take an interest in her welfare was intoxicating. Or was it just the liquor talking?

When they got back to her dorm room, Grant deposited Shari on her perfectly made-up bed, which was right next to Dina's unmade one. He settled her in the bed and then stood.

"I hate to leave you here unattended," he said, looking around at the half-neat, half-unkempt room as if he was afraid to leave her alone.

"Then don't leave," Shari said, staring at him openly. "Stay awhile."

"Okay." He sat back down on her bed with his hands clutched in his lap.

An hour later, after they'd chatted about classes and campus gossip, Grant stood up to leave since Shari appeared somewhat sober.

"Wait!" Shari sat up on her knees, wrapped her arms around his neck and kissed him. Grant appeared taken aback as if he hadn't seen that coming, so Shari pulled away. "Do you think I'm ugly?" she asked, frowning. She felt foolish for kissing him.

"Of course not."

"Just not pretty enough to kiss?" Shari inquired. She slumped back down onto her hunches on the bed. "Is that why you didn't kiss me back? Is something wrong with me? I mean, even my so-called boyfriend, Thomas, won't kiss me and we're supposed to be dating."

"That's not it at all." Grant glanced down and pushed back a tiny strand of hair that had fallen in Shari's face and then stroked her cheek. And as if trying to reassure her, he kissed her. It wasn't a simple kiss, either. It was a kiss meant to illicit passion. And it did. The kiss turned pretty quickly into something more. Next thing she knew, Grant was pushing her back onto the bed and lowering himself on top of her. He gathered her close in his arms, and she gripped his head with both her hands and kissed him back in an explosion of passion.

Grant stroked her lips over and over with his, thrusting his tongue in and out of her mouth. His hands wandered over her back and derriere, bringing her closer to his hardness. She didn't stop him when he began unbuttoning her shirt and tossed it aside. Nor did she stop him when he began palming her breasts or reached behind her and unsnapped her bra. She was fully involved in the kiss and it was inciting all the harbored attraction she'd had for him. She could hear his breathing becoming labored. She wanted more.

But Grant broke the kiss and lifted his head.

"Why did you stop?" Shari asked, looking up at him. She knew he wanted her because the lower half of his body was straining in his jeans against her. And the sensual tension that was mounting inside her was like nothing she'd ever felt before. Her senses were acutely aware of Grant. How he tasted slightly salty from the chips and beer at the party. How he smelled spicy and musky. And he felt...well, his hair wasn't coarse like some men. It felt like fine silk and she wanted to continue running her fingers through it. Hell, she could go on kissing him forever. "I don't want you to stop." She reached for him again. "I want this. I want you."

Grant seemed to be warring with himself, and Shari could sense it. She could see the intense heat in his jade eyes, and it excited her to see the passion lying in them. To help him along, Shari leaned in and traced a teasing path with her tongue from his neck and up to his ear before sucking on it. Grant groaned aloud and she knew she'd found his sensitive spot. She had him right where she wanted him, and there was no turning back. She couldn't believe she was being so bold, so daring, but she wanted this man. She slid into his lap and ground her body against him, causing a thrilling sensation to form between her legs.

Shari felt the moment Grant's resolve dissipated because his tongue dove inside her mouth to duel with hers, causing Shari to shiver deliciously. Then his palm found its way back to one plump breast and he bent down to suck on the globe. Shari forgot to breathe. Instead, she arched against him, eager for more.

Grant quickly began undressing her, unzipping her jeans and slowly pulling them and her panties off in one swift motion. It wasn't long before was he was naked beside her. Kissing her. Touching her. Tasting her. She purred in her throat when Grant entered her and began moving inside her. She'd barely even felt the slight pain as Grant broke through her virgin barrier and neither, apparently, had he. The exquisite slowness of Grant's thrusting stirred all her emotions and Shari moaned aloud. Pleasure coiled through her, slow and deep, causing tension to build so much so that Shari thought she would go up in flames at any moment. And she did.

Blissfully pulsing, their orgasms came almost simultaneously, draining them until they both fell languid on her bed. Softly, tenderly, Grant reached over and stroked her cheek. Shari felt tranquil and at peace for the first time in her life. Her first time had been with Grant and had been everything she could have hoped for. As she drifted off to sleep, she hoped they would have this moment again someday.

"What the hell?" Dina said from the doorway of their dorm room the following morning.

Shari wiped the sleep from her eyes and peered across at Dina and then at Grant, who was rising beside her, bare chested and all. Dina must have stayed out the night before if she was just returning home. Shari reached across and pulled a sheet across her naked body.

"I think we all know what happened," Grant said sheepishly from her side. "Could you be so kind as to give us some privacy, Dina?"

"I guess I have no choice," she said haughtily, slamming the door behind her.

Once she'd gone, Grant sprinted out of Shari's bed, dressed and ducked out the room. He was gone so fast that Shari hadn't been able to tell him just how much she'd enjoyed herself.

The following day was worse because as soon as he saw her, Shari noticed how embarrassed Grant looked. Gone was the easy camaraderie they'd shared before they'd slept together, and in its place was a weird awkwardness that she didn't know how to combat. She sought to alleviate his fears by making light of their night together.

"Listen, Grant," she said after class ended and the room had cleared. "About last night…"

"I am so sorry I allowed things to go as far as they did—"

"There's no need for you to feel sorry," Shari said, interrupting him. "We're good. Last night was just a hookup." She looked down as she spoke. It was a lie, but she didn't know what else to say. "We're still friends. Nothing has to change. I don't want you to feel like you owe me anything."

"What?" Grant was floored. He hadn't expected this reaction. He wanted to see if Shari forgave him for behaving so selfishly and taking what he wanted regardless of whether it was the right thing to do. He was hoping she would give him another chance to start fresh and take her out on a proper date. He desperately wanted to see her on a permanent basis, but it was clear she felt differently. And it crushed him.

"I…I don't want you to feel….you know…bad," Shari reiterated, fumbling over her words. "What's done is done. I just hope it doesn't ruin our friendship."

"Uh, okay," Grant conceded. He couldn't believe Shari was being this coldhearted about the intimacy they'd shared. Could he have been wrong about her all along? Perhaps around campus they had it wrong. Shari was the heartless bitch and Dina was the nice one. "If that's the way you want it."

"I do." Shari offered her hand. "Friends?"

"Friends." Grant took her hand and shook it reluctantly.

Shari wished she could say the same about her roommate. Two months later, she caught Dina and Grant in the courtyard holding hands and whispering softly into each other's ear.

"No, no, no." She shook her head and ducked behind a column so the duo wouldn't see her. Shari wiped away the tears rolling down her cheeks at seeing her best friend betray her. Surely Dina wouldn't steal the man she'd adored. The man with whom she'd shared her first time. It was girlfriend code. You never dated a man your friend had been with or wanted. She'd told Dina how she felt about Grant. Why would Dina do this to her?

The answer came to her like someone had dropped a ton of bricks over her head. Nausea rose up in Shari's throat and she clutched her mouth. Ohmigod. Dina had wanted Grant all along and was merely humoring Shari's deluded fantasies. It must have really gotten her goat that Shari had managed to get Grant in her bed. So she'd turned on the charm and made sure Shari would never have a chance with Grant again. How could she have been a fool this entire time? How had she not seen who Dina truly was?

Shari rushed into the bathroom in the Business Administration hall, but that didn't stop her bout of nausea. Nothing did. Several hours later, she was staring at the nurse in the Health Clinic.

"When was your last period?" the nurse inquired, jotting down some notes.

Dread rushed through Shari. Her period. Her mind raced to the last time she recalled having it. Two weeks before her one-night stand with Grant. She hadn't had one since, hadn't even thought about it because she'd been trying to push down her feelings for Grant. Her hand flew to her mouth.

The nurse looked at her. "So we need a pregnancy test, then?"

# Chapter 1

"Our cake is a visual masterpiece," Shari told her cousin, Carter Drayson, the artisan cake maker for Lillian's Bakery, and the black sheep of the family. They stood in a large studio kitchen with cameras in front of them. "It's by far the best cake. We are going to win this."

Shari glanced behind her to look at the four-tier champagne cake before finally setting her eyes on her nemesis Dina English's cake from Brown Sugar Bakery.

Dina was standing there, looking poised and sophisticated in designer duds, making Shari feel dowdy in her jeans and Lillian's Bakery T-shirt. But that was okay, because Lillian's was the better bakery. Not only had Dina stolen Grant Robinson, Shari's first love, and run off with him to get married, but she'd stolen Lillian's recipes for her own bakery. And Shari felt responsible.

When Shari and Dina had attended Ledgeman University together, Grandma Lillian had taken a liking to Dina almost immediately and offered her a summer job after freshman year. While in college, Dina had continued to work at Lillian's during the summers. Shari had hoped that she and Dina would work side by side at the bakery after graduation. They'd been a great team. With Shari's background in business and Dina's finesse, they would have been unstoppable. Shari would have finally risen to the top in her family instead of always feeling like a dimly lit planet among her confident, smart cousins, the real stars of the Drayson clan. But life had thrown her a curveball when Dina had left to create her own bakery.

Five years later and Shari had never truly recovered from the betrayal. How could she when Dina had married her son's father and prevented them from ever being a real family?

"We got this," Carter said confidently. He had an arrogant swag about him that Shari sometimes envied.

*You Take the Cake*'s host came over and stood between the two bakeries and said, "And the winner is... Brown Sugar Bakery!" Applause erupted from the live audience, and Shari's heart deflated.

*How can this be?* Shari looked over at Brown Sugar's creation. The cake was at best ordinary.

Dina came over and laughed. "That's right, Shari. I win again."

Shari rushed over to the host of the show and grabbed his arm. "There has to be a mistake. She should be disqualified."

"Why? What's wrong?" the host asked.

"The whole world should know what kind of person Dina English is." Shari turned and glared at Dina. "She traded on our nearly four-year friendship, turned her back on my family's bakery and then stole the man I loved. You can't let her win!"

Dina smirked and gave Shari a pitiful look as she walked toward her. "You're so pathetic. Can't you see? I've already won."

Shari looked down, but not before seeing, to her horror, Dina holding her son, Andre, in her arms and carrying him away. "Noooo!"

Shari woke up with a start and her eyes popped open. She was surprised to find her four-year-old son, Andre, peering down at her. He was wearing his favorite Spiderman pajamas and was holding his stuffed animal, Wiggles. "Mama, are you okay? Were you having a bad dream? You were yelling awfully loud."

"I must've been, baby." Shari sat upright, throwing the down comforter back off and pulling Andre into a bear hug. "I'm sorry if Mommy scared you." She glanced at herself in the mirror. The wrap she'd been wearing on her hair had come off, and her hair was a tangled mess. Add the old tank top and pajama bottoms she was wearing and it was no wonder she couldn't find a man.

"Are you sure you're okay?" Andre's expressive green eyes looked into her brown ones, eager for reassurance.

"I'm fine, I'm fine." Shari scooped him up in her arms, slid on her slippers and padded off into the kitchen to make him some breakfast.

"Can I have Cocoa Puffs?" Andre asked when they reached her large, country-style eat-in kitchen.

It might be modest to some, but her two-bedroom

bungalow in Chicago's Glenville Heights was just perfect for her and Andre. Since she loved to cook, she had added modern white cabinets and appliances, including a flat-top stove, double-sided refrigerator and a dishwasher.

"Are you sure?" Shari inquired. "Because I was going to make chocolate chip pancakes, but if you'd rather cereal…" She shrugged her shoulders and waited for the response she knew was coming.

Andre shook his head. "No, I want pancakes! With lots of syrup."

Shari smiled. "Sure thing." She lowered him into a chair at the pedestal table.

She pulled the pancake mix and chocolate chip morsels out of the pantry and the milk and eggs out of the fridge. Usually, she would make them from scratch, but she needed to get to the bakery.

A couple of months ago, her grandmother, Lillian Reynolds-Drayson, had informed her children and grandchildren that she'd signed the bakery up to participate in a reality TV Show called *You Take the Cake.* On the show, bakeries were asked to perform culinary feats, and at stake was a $100,000 prize. Last year's winners had become overnight sensations and their bakery had gained national prominence. For two months, the entire Drayson clan had been looking at recipes and cake designs in the show's "Around the World" theme to blow the competition away.

Her grandmother had made quite a speech about how they had to stop all the backbiting and work together as a family. She indicated she would soon be passing the business to one of her grandchildren. The decision wasn't going to be an easy one. They were all qualified to run Lillian's. They'd all started learning the business from the bottom up, delivering cakes, working the dock and cleaning the store.

Shari knew she had tough competition from her cousins for the position. Shari, Drake, Belinda and Carter all considered themselves the best bakers in the shop. No wonder Grandma Lillian couldn't decide among them.

Her cousin Belinda, Aunt Daisy's daughter, excelled at everything she did whether it was school or baking. Somehow, she made it all look effortless. Belinda always dressed smartly in designer clothes and didn't go out of the house without her full makeup and her long black hair ironed bone straight. Now, she'd hooked one-time basketball pro and Lillian's baker, Malik Anthony. Belinda was now set to be the first of her cousins to marry.

Then there was Belinda's brother Drake. He knew marketing and social media better than any of them. Drake, Malik and Carter had started a blog called "Brothers Who Bake" that offered recipes and advice and was attracting a wide audience. The success of the blog had inspired them to write a cookbook that was now under contract with a major publishing house.

Last but not least, there was Carter Drayson, Lillian's artisan cake maker and a real charmer. Up until recently, her cousin had been a true ladies' man just like his father, Uncle Devon, who'd never married. But then her tall, handsome cousin had gotten hit by the love bug last month. And on top of that, Carter was the most sought-after cake designer at Lillian's. Shari couldn't help but be a little resentful of her older cousin. She, too, was an equally skilled baker and designer, but she had to admit no one could create artistry on cakes quite like him.

Shari knew she was good, but in a family of stars, it was hard carving out her piece of the pie. She was not as confident as Belinda, as technically savvy as Drake or as skilled as Carter, but she deserved a shot to run Lillian's. Her business degree was evidence of that and she had come up with the idea to package Lillian's cake mixes. But somehow her baby sister, Monica, had taken over running the cake mix business; she just had to prove to Grandma Lillian that she had what it took to be a leader.

Two hours later, Shari and Andre walked from the parking garage where she had a reserved spot to the front of Lillian's on North Michigan Avenue. Shari smiled as she always did when she saw the marble facade standing out from the other Magnificent Mile designer boutiques. Her grandparents owned the entire sixteen-story building, which included a slew of offices on floors two through sixteen, while Lillian's Bakery spanned the entire first floor.

*Lillian's* was written in large, gold, script lettering on the storefront windows through which passersby gazed at ornate wedding cakes and lavish cake designs. Some might say the cakes, cookies and other sumptuous desserts looked like fancy pieces of jewelry or handbags, but the best part was that they were edible.

Lillian's had been a Chicago staple since the 1960s when her grandparents had opened their first storefront in Hyde Park. Their love story was one Shari would never forget. Her grandmother, Lillian Reynolds-Drayson, was a widowed single mother whose husband,

Jack Reynolds, died of a heart attack. Shari's father, Dwight, had only been a year old at the time. Grandpa Henry had arrived a few years later and patiently wooed her grandmother until she'd finally let her guard down. They were married soon after and Grandpa Henry adopted her father. As for the business, the rest, as they say, was history.

Shari couldn't help but think of that story every time she entered Lillian's. Today was no exception, even as she rushed inside because she was a few minutes late. Andre had lost his favorite toy, and they'd been unable to leave the house until he'd found it.

The store always brought a smile to her face. Her grandparents had spared no expense with the decor. It screamed opulence and elegance. Rich mahogany woodwork shined throughout the store while the crystal chandeliers sparkled like brilliant diamonds. Ribbons of copper and gold were inlaid in the glistening marble countertops and matched the ambiance of the various boutiques on the Magnificent Mile, where only the rich and famous shopped.

Grandpa Henry was working the front counter and retail area when she arrived. His hair was shock full of gray and he was dressed in a Tommy Bahama shirt and trousers. "You're late, Shari," he said. "Everyone's already here."

"I know, Grandpa," Shari responded. "Can you watch Andre while I go into the meeting?"

"Of course, darling." Grandpa Henry smiled down at his great-grandson. "Come with great-grandpa." He held out his hand and Andre took it.

Shari rushed down the hallway past the framed photographs of Lillian's through the years. Her grandmother had been a real looker in her heyday. Even now, she was tall and slim with caramel skin, and her face held nary a wrinkle even though she was approaching eighty. There was a picture of Grandma Lillian holding Shari's father, Dwight, in front of the first storefront in Hyde Park, another of the grand opening of the Mag Mile location, but Shari's favorite was the Drayson family picture when Lillian's was featured in a local magazine a year ago.

She walked past the kitchen to the adjacent executive office area, which included a conference room, and found the entire Drayson family already gathered around a large square table with high-backed chairs.

"Hello, hello." Shari gave a quick smile to her grandmother, who was sitting at the head of the table, while Aunt Daisy and Uncle Devon, her cousins and Belinda's fiancé, Malik, sat flanking each other. Shari nodded at her father and her sister Monica before sliding into an open chair.

"So happy you could join us," Grandma Lillian said reproachfully.

Shari shrugged. "Andre was a handful this morning."

"When isn't Andre a handful?" Carter said fondly from across the table.

Shari knew Carter adored his little cousin and the feeling was mutual. Andre looked up to his "uncle" Carter. She supposed Andre had a special place in his heart because he was a little bit mischievous and probably reminded Carter of himself.

Shari's sister Monica laughed. "This is true." Watching Andre was not an easy task, Shari knew, and because Monica was so short at five foot three, and Andre was really tall for his age, Monica found him to be a handful.

"Well, as you know, the *You Take the Cake* competition is almost upon us," Lillian said. "I'd like to know what recipes and plans you've come up with to ensure Lillian's the win."

Everyone started talking all at once, eager to impress Grandma Lillian with their recipes. "One at a time, please," she admonished, holding up her hand.

As usual, Drake was the first to speak. Adjusting his gold-rimmed glasses, he explained, "Carter, Malik and I have come up with a number of great recipes."

Her cousin Drake had a medium build that was always dressed in trendy clothes. Today he wore a military jacket, jeans, an oxford shirt and Timberland boots. He looked like perfection. And he always thought he was right.

Belinda spoke next. "And I've been collaborating with Malik here—" she turned to give her fiancé a wink "—on a couple of wedding cake designs."

Grandma Lillian turned to Shari. "Shari, how about you?"

All eyes in the room turned to Shari and she swallowed hard.

"I have some ideas, too," she offered, "using unconventional ingredients in the cakes. You know, the show is known for its mystery ingredients."

"That sounds great, dear," Grandma Lillian said. "Sounds like everyone's come to the table with something."

"I think we should do a dry run of the recipes," her father added. "We should start today."

His booming baritone voice, not to mention the touch

of gray at his temples, lent him an air of dominance. Everyone quickly nodded their assent to his suggestion.

"Good. If there's nothing else…" Grandma Lillian began, but Carter interrupted her.

"Well, actually there is," Carter said.

"Oh, please, Carter," Grandma Lillian said. "Please tell me you haven't broken that young girl's heart."

Carter had been dating socialite Lorraine Hawthorne-Hayes for about five weeks. They'd even made the paper a couple of times. Lorraine was not Carter's typical woman. Yes, she was beautiful, but she dressed in classic fashions unlike the flashier women he usually dated. Lorraine was the daughter of Arnold and Abigail Hawthorne-Hayes of Hawthorne-Hayes Jewelers. The Hawthorne-Hayes family was Chicago royalty and easily outranked the Draysons. Everyone in the family was waiting for Carter to say he'd tired of Lorraine and moved on to the next woman.

Shari hoped not. She'd warned Carter about breaking Lorraine's heart.

"Actually quite the opposite," Carter responded, smiling from ear to ear. "Lorraine and I are engaged."

"Get out!" Devon jumped up out of his chair and faced his son. "You! Engaged?"

"That's right, Dad." Carter laughed. "I'm not going to be a perennial bachelor like you."

"Congratulations, Carter." Shari leaned over and gave him a playful punch while Malik and Drake reached across the table and shook his hand affectionately.

"That's wonderful news," Grandma Lillian replied. "Two grandchildren engaged this year!" She glanced at

Belinda and Carter, and then at Shari. "I hope everyone will follow your example."

Shari lowered her head. She knew that comment was directed at her. Her family had been disappointed when she'd had Andre out of wedlock. She'd tarnished the Drayson family name, but Shari didn't care. She would do it again a thousand times over. She loved Andre and wouldn't trade him for anything in the world.

"Don't worry, kid," Carter whispered in Shari's ear. "She's only using you as a whipping boy because I'm finally out of the doghouse. Keep your head up."

"Oh, I don't regret having my son for a second," Shari replied. It was the one decision she'd been clear on from the moment she'd discovered she was pregnant.

Carter motioned with his hands for everyone to quiet down. "I'm not finished yet. I have other news."

"As if your engagement isn't news enough," his best friend, Malik, replied laughing.

Carter rolled his eyes. "You all know that I was approached by a New York restaurateur who offered me the job of executive baker for his operation, but have decided to stay."

"No, I didn't know. Who's this restaurateur who tried to steal you away from us?" Shari asked. Despite his playboy ways, Shari knew that Andre was attached to his "uncle" Carter and she was glad he wasn't leaving Chicago.

Carter turned to Shari. "Does the name Grant Robinson ring a bell?"

All color rushed out of Shari's face at hearing Grant's name again after all this time, and her eyes widened in alarm. "Uh, I think I remember him," she finally managed to eke out. "Did he say anything about me?"

"He didn't say much," Carter replied. "He only mentioned that you two went to college together and that he couldn't wait to catch up on old times."

Like that was even possible, Shari thought. Clearly what she and Grant had shared together had meant nothing to him. How could he think of her so casually as if they'd never slept together?

Carter continued, interrupting her thoughts. "Grant indicated that even if I chose to turn the job down, there might be an opportunity with Lillian's to supply the desserts to his restaurant chain. He's on his way here now."

Grant was coming to Lillian's? Shari was frozen speechless. She hadn't seen the man since she'd graduated from Ledgeman University, and he'd broken her heart by marrying her former best friend and college roommate, Dina English.

"Sounds promising," her father said. "I'd like to meet him."

Her father, Dwight, had taken over the business aspects of the Drayson Corporation while her uncle Devon focused on the real-estate end of the family business. The Drayson family had leveraged their income from the family business and invested wisely in Chicago real estate. Their real-estate interests had made them multi-millionaires.

"Absolutely," Carter said and then glanced at Shari.

Shari felt like she was going to be physically ill. "If you'll excuse me…" She rushed out of the conference room, ran to the unisex restroom and locked the door firmly behind her. Shari tried to take deep, calming breaths to steady her nerves, but she was having a hard time catching her breath. Her breathing was shallow and uneasy at the thought of meeting her son's father face-to-face after five years.

Everyone in the family thought Thomas Abernathy, the guy Shari had dated casually in college, was Andre's father and despised him for leaving her high and dry. They couldn't be more wrong. Thomas had been a good friend who'd accompanied her to social events, but they'd never been together sexually. Shari had always suspected he was gay, but it wasn't until she'd come clean about sleeping with Grant that he'd dropped the bomb and admitted that he was indeed gay. But the poor thing refused to come out of the closet to his family. Shari wasn't about to force his hand, so she'd allowed the Drayson family to believe he was Andre's father when in fact, Grant Robinson was Andre's dad.

How was she going to face Grant after all this time? And how would she be able to keep Andre out of his sight?

## Chapter 2

"We're here, sir," the driver of Grant Robinson's town car said when they arrived in front of Lillian's. Grant glanced out of the window. He'd come to Chicago under the guise of speaking with Carter Drayson about the possibility of having Lillian's desserts sold at Robinson Restaurants, but that wasn't his only reason for coming. He was dying to see Shari Drayson again.

What had it been? Five years since he'd seen her last? A day hadn't gone by when he hadn't thought of her pretty face, large brown eyes and ample curves. He'd been attracted to Shari since they'd gone to Ledgeman University and had been in the same study group, but then they'd settled into an easy friendship.

It wasn't until that fateful night at a frat party that their relationship had taken a sudden and interesting turn. After a grueling midterm exam, their study group had gone out partying and Shari had really tied one on. His intent had been to take her home, put her to bed and go home. Instead, emboldened by the liquor, Shari had planted a kiss on him that had stirred his hidden passions. He'd acted on his lust and made love to her.

The next morning, he'd regretted taking advantage of her while she was inebriated, but she'd been so cute and sexy wearing a cutoff T-shirt and fitted jeans that his hormones had taken over. He would have preferred to have courted Shari properly, taken her out to the movies or to dinner. And he would have done so, finally revealing his true feelings for her without alcohol clouding their judgment. Instead, Shari had told him what they'd shared had been a casual hookup between friends and that he didn't owe her anything.

Worse yet, her roommate and his ex-wife, Dina English, had caught them in bed together, which only added to the awkward situation. After that, Dina had turned up the heat and made a play for him, and without Shari giving him any sign of interest, he'd given in to Dina's incessant flirting.

*Big mistake.* Grant should never have gotten involved with Dina. Truth be told, Dina was a salve for his broken heart after Shari. He'd thought the fact that they'd made love would have changed their friendship into something more serious, but it hadn't. So when Dina had shown genuine interest in him, he'd gotten caught up in the adoration. Then, of course, there was the pressure from his father to settle down and get focused. His father had indicated he wouldn't pass the family restaurants over to him until he was married.

His parents owned a slew of soul-food restaurants across the country, and Grant was poised to run them—

if he found a wife. And so, when Dina convinced him
to go to Las Vegas soon after graduation, they'd gotten hitched. Of course, his parents hadn't been happy.
They'd expected a large ceremony full of pomp and cir-
cumstance. It didn't matter, though, because his marriage had lasted less than a year.

Why? Because Grant had regretted the decision
almost instantly. Marrying Dina had been one of the
poorest decisions of his life. Worse, he'd resented his
father, Warren Robinson, for forcing him into a loveless marriage. As soon as he was able, he'd started his
own restaurant specializing in New American cuisine.
One restaurant had turned into two and so on and so
on. Now he owned a chain of Robinson Restaurants
across the East Coast.

Regrets. Missed opportunities. Lost time. Those
were the words he thought of when he thought about
Shari Drayson. But no more. He'd come here today to
find out if there was a chance to recapture the passion
they'd shared that one night. Now that time had passed,
Grant was sure that his emotion hadn't been one-sided,
that Shari had to have felt it, too. This time he wasn't
walking away until he found out.

Grant pulled on the brass-plated door handle and
walked inside. When he did, he was overcome with
the aroma of freshly baked goods. His nose savored
the sweet smell, and his eyes grew large as he looked
around the showroom. He was impressed by the crystal
chandeliers, marble floors and counters, but even more
so by the delectable treats, pastries, brownies, maca-
roons and cakes aligned in the display counter. He'd
come here to see Shari and Carter, but first he had to
have a taste of one of these sweet treats.

\* \* \*

Shari couldn't stay in the bathroom forever. Otherwise, her family would get suspicious and come looking for her. She stared at herself in the mirror. She was in no way ready to see Grant Robinson again. Look at her! The "mom clothes" she wore every day—blue jeans and a simple white peasant shirt cinched at the waist—didn't scream sexy by any means.

To make matters worse, she had no makeup on other than some lip gloss. Whenever she was baking in the kitchen, she preferred to keep it simple and comfortable.

When she emerged from the bathroom, her family had dispersed in different directions, and she was on her way back to the conference room for her purse, in the hopes that her foundation compact was in it, when a baritone voice said from behind her, "Shari? Is that you?"

Her heart went pitter-pat. Slowly, Shari turned on her heel and looked up to find Grant standing next to Carter and smiling down at her. She'd forgotten how tall he was. He was at least six feet, and those dimples and green eyes… Now, those she remembered…because she saw them every day looking back at her. On her son's face.

Grant was still sexier than any man had a right to be. He was wearing a stylish suit with Italian loafers and a blue striped tie. He was the picture of a successful businessman. He'd clearly achieved what he'd set out to do when he'd obtained his MBA at Ledgeman.

Before she could speak, Grant pulled her firmly against him for a warm hug. He didn't immediately let go, allowing Shari to smell his musky, masculine scent.

She eventually was the one to pull away, and she

looked up at him with an open, friendly smile. "Grant, it's good to see you again."

"You, too." He grinned broadly.

Shari sighed inwardly. The years had been good to Grant. And he looked even more handsome, more distinguished than he did back in college. Her inner muscles churned, letting her know that the tug she'd felt years ago hadn't dissipated and was still strong—no... stronger than before.

Shari came out of her daze and noticed that Carter and Grant had moved away, so she shuffled after them. Carter was introducing Grant to the rest of the family in the kitchen. Her father, especially, seemed very impressed with Grant's success.

"Well, I for one don't appreciate you trying to steal a member of my family away," Grandma Lillian said from over by the massive table where she, Belinda, Malik and Drake were working on one of the wedding cake designs for the *You Take The Cake* competition.

When had they gotten started? Shari wondered. Probably when she was in the restroom for half an hour trying to figure out how she was going to handle being in the same room as Grant again. *Why is it that he still has the same effect on me as he did when I was twenty?* It still felt like he'd taken up all the air in the room, which was why she was having a hard time breathing again.

Shari tried to focus her thoughts when Grant turned to her and asked, "So everyone knows I tried to steal Carter?"

Shari nodded.

"Well, it was a worth a shot," Grant said, turning back around to answer Mrs. Reynolds-Drayson's question. "But after seeing this operation—" he motioned around the kitchen "—I can see why he wouldn't leave. Your family is pretty amazing, which is why I have a proposition for you."

Grandma Lillian eyed Grant suspiciously. She was wary of strangers, especially someone trying to steal one of her cubs.

"But first, I need Shari for a moment." Grant pulled Shari away from the kitchen and into the conference room. "I was hoping we could talk."

"About?" Shari could only muster one word sentences when in Grant's presence.

"About what happened that night between us," Grant said, shifting uncomfortably from side to side. He hated to bring it up, but he had to clear the air.

Shari looked at the door. She didn't want any of her cousins to overhear the conversation. "Grant, I don't think this is the time or place—"

Grant interrupted her as if he hadn't heard a word she said. "I always thought you were a great girl, Shari. I still do. I just hope you don't hold it against me that I took advantage of you that night and behaved so abominably."

Shari wasn't sure how to react to Grant's apology. Maybe she wouldn't have held it against him, if he hadn't jumped from her bed into her best friend's. But was it all his fault? She had told him that night that there were "no strings attached." Even so, that didn't change the fact that he'd rushed off into Dina's arms and married the woman.

"So how's Dina?" Shari inquired, her voice holding a touch of bitterness. She couldn't allow herself to get caught up in Grant again.

Grant's face darkened. "I wouldn't know. We're divorced, and I haven't spoken to her in years."

Shari's heart leapt. *He was divorced!* When? Why? For how long?

"Mommy, Mommy!" Andre came bounding down the hall toward her. Shari bent down and he flew into her arms. Her heart began hammering furiously in her chest. She hadn't been prepared for this introduction so quickly. She had no choice but to introduce her son to Grant and pray for the best. Perhaps he wouldn't realize her secret…that Andre was his.

# Chapter 3

"Andre, Mommy would like you to meet one of her old friends," Shari said, turning and looking up at Grant, who was looking at her strangely. Was he surprised that she had a child? "Andre, this is Grant Robinson."

Grant looked at Shari curiously for several moments, but didn't say a word. Instead, he squatted down and shook hands with the little man.

Shari was floored. What should she do next? Should she say, *by the way, this is your son?*

"Nice to meet you," Andre replied, shaking Grant's hand. Shari's throat constricted as she watched father and son interact for the first time.

"How long have you known my mommy?"

"A very long time," Shari replied for Grant.

Grant rose to his feet. "He's beautiful, Shari."

"Thank you."

Shari didn't get to say anything more because Grandpa Henry came over to meet Grant. "Sorry, Shari," Grandpa Henry apologized. "Andre got away from me up front. But I hear Mr. Robinson here is interested in Lillian's and your father asked me to come get him about a proposition."

Grandpa Henry grasped Grant by the shoulder and pulled him toward the executive office where her father and grandmother were waiting. "Let's discuss some business."

Shari walked out of the conference room and watched the men walk down the hall. She felt an impending sense of doom that all was not right with the world because there was no way that having Grant Robinson back in her life was going to end with a good result.

Andre poked her in the leg. "Is everything okay, Mommy?"

"Of course." Shari bent down to pick him up. "Mommy's got everything under control."

"Are you sure about that?" Belinda whispered in Shari's ear once Grant had walked off. "He's pretty handsome. Not to mention sexy."

Shari whirled around with Andre, the evidence of just how sexy Grant really was. She lowered their son to the ground. "Honey, why don't you go to the kitchen and get a snack from one of your uncles?" Where had Belinda come from, anyway? She hadn't even heard her sneak up.

Andre rushed off toward the kitchen to find Drake, Carter or Malik, whom he considered like uncles.

"You guys know each other, right?" Belinda asked.

"Because his name sounds oddly familiar, like I've heard it before."

Shari nodded. "We went to college together."

"Oh, yes, now I remember." Belinda eyes sparked with interest. "He's the one you had a crush on, isn't he?"

"One and the same. And then he went off and married Dina." Shari tried not to sound bitter, but it was hard not to, knowing what Dina took from her—the chance to be with the father of her child.

Belinda's mouth formed an *O* as if the light had finally dawned. "He married Dina? Well, that hits close to home."

"You have no idea," Shari murmured underneath her breath.

"Do you guys share some sort of history other than the Dina connection?" Belinda wondered aloud.

Shari eyed her suspiciously. Had she given something away? Was she sending off vibes that there was more to the story? "Why are you bringing this up?" She evaded the question rather than lie to her cousin.

Belinda shrugged. "Oh, no reason. I was just curious."

Shari breathed a sigh of relief. "All right. Well, let's go bake some cakes." She left Belinda in the hall and walked ahead of her toward the kitchen. She didn't want anyone to realize the true connection between her and Grant. But would that even be possible now that Grant had met Andre?

Grant eventually left Shari's father and went in search of the lady herself. Although the older man seemed intent on talking about a business venture between the two companies, Grant's mind's was far from thinking about it. Yes, he was interested in having Lillian's desserts exclusively in his restaurants, but after seeing Shari again and meeting her son, all bets were off.

He'd calculated the young boy's age in his head and he had to be four or five at the most, which meant Shari had gotten pregnant in college. Was she pregnant when she'd slept with him? He recalled that she'd been dating some guy named Thomas. Was he Andre's father? Or worse yet, could Andre be *his?*

As soon as the thought popped in his head, Grant quickly dismissed it. If Andre was his, he'd lost years of his son's life, those early primary years when a son needed his father. Grant felt sick at the thought. Surely, Shari wouldn't have kept Andre from him. Could she be that vindictive? He had started dating Dina soon after their encounter. Had Shari been so upset with him that she'd calculatingly decided to keep him from his child?

Grant had to know.

He found Shari in the kitchen with her family. He watched her from the doorway. What he'd always liked about Shari was that she wasn't aware of her beauty. She was unpretentious. Always had been. Her dark brown hair was swept back in a long ponytail. She wore very little makeup other than some lipstick, but she was still the prettiest girl in the room. And her figure, although she was hiding behind a white shirt and baggy jeans, was just as curvy as Grant remembered. He closed his eyes for a second and recalled her full breasts and voluptuous behind. He would like nothing more than to smack it. Grant's eyes popped open at the visual. He was daydreaming about what it would be like to make love with Shari again, even when he knew she could have kept a monumental secret from him for years. What was wrong with him?

He returned his focus back to Shari. She'd donned an apron over her jeans and it was splattered with flour, and she held a pastry bag in her hand that she was using to adorn a cake on a board. The entire family was working together as a team for some competition they were discussing. He wished he had the same camaraderie with his own family, but the Robinson bunch didn't show affection toward each other. His father was a cold-hearted businessman with a heart of a stone; he only cared about the bottom line. And his mother…well, she was a borderline drunk. Often in his youth, he'd find her passed out on the sofa after one too many vodka tonics. He barely spoke to his parents now. As an only child, he envied Shari her big family.

But if Andre was his, Grant was going to be a part of the Drayson family soon enough. And there was only one way to find out.

Shari glanced up and sucked in a deep breath. Grant was watching her from the kitchen doorway. When he saw that she'd caught him, he motioned her over. Reluctantly, Shari held the pastry bag out to Belinda. "You want to take over?"

Shari inclined her head toward the door, and Belinda smiled knowingly. "Just because I'm going to go talk to him, don't go getting ideas," Shari whispered.

"Who, me?" Belinda asked innocently.

Shari walked over to Grant and nodded when he said, "Sorry to disturb you, but do you have a moment?"

She glanced behind her to see several curious pairs

of eyes staring at them. Her family was such nosy busy-
bodies. "Yes, follow me." She led him back into the conference room. "Was there something else?"

"Well, yes," Grant said. "I was hoping you were free
tonight for dinner."

"Dinner?" She hadn't expected that.

"I thought we could catch up," Grant said. "You
know, reminisce about old times. How about I pick you
up around seven?"

"Well…I don't know. There's Andre to think about,"
Shari began, but Grant refused to take no for an answer.

"With a family as large as this one, I'm sure you can
find a babysitter. So what's your address?"

Several minutes later, Shari had written down her
address, handed it to Grant and arranged for babysit-
ting all in one fell swoop. She was going out on a date
with Grant Robinson.

Shari paced the floor of her home on Chicago's north
side in Glenville Heights waiting for Grant's arrival. She
hadn't been out on a date in over two years. Most men
her age weren't interested in dating a single mother and
so she'd become accustomed to staying home, curled up
in front of the television or reading a good book while
Andre played.

But her date tonight was much different than any of
her other encounters. She was going out with Grant. The
man she'd crushed on for years only to share a fateful
one-night stand with him that had resulted in the love
of her life, Andre. Was this really a date? she wondered.
Grant had claimed he was asking her out to catch up
with an old friend. Was she reading too much into it?

In any event, she'd dropped Andre off at her parents'

and so the night was hers to spend as she saw fit. Shari was a mix of emotions. Excitement. Nervousness. And fear. Fear that Grant might somehow realize the truth. But why would he? Everyone in the family assumed Andre's father was Thomas Abernathy. They all assumed that when she told Thomas she was pregnant, he'd broken up with her.

Shari knew her family was completely off the mark. Andre's father was gorgeous, sexy, smart, millionaire Grant Robinson. A man she'd never fully gotten over, and now she was about to spend the evening with him.

She'd debated with herself on what to wear, but had finally settled on a simple V-neck, sleeveless, jersey wrap dress. It showed a hint of cleavage, but not too much. She paired it with hoop earrings and simple sling-back sandals. She couldn't wear stilettos like her little sister Monica and would probably fall over if she tried. It was the best she could do with short notice and her meager wardrobe. Monica and Belinda were always telling her to spruce up her appearance if she wanted to find a man, but Shari liked her jeans. Plus, she couldn't pull off the hip Forever 21 clothes and stilettos like Monica or the designer clothes like Belinda.

Luckily, she didn't have too long to wonder if her outfit was good enough because Grant arrived promptly at 7:00 p.m. When she opened the door, Grant was holding a bouquet of roses.

"For me?" Shari touched her chest.

"Of course." Grant handed the flowers to her. Then his eyes gave her an appreciative once-over from head to toe. He must have liked the canary-yellow dress she was wearing because he commented, "You look beautiful tonight, Shari, but then again, you always did."

Shari blushed furiously. His compliment gave her butterflies and she was luxuriating in the moment, which was why they stood there for several more awkward moments in the foyer, both looking at each other, before Grant finally asked, "May I come in?"

Shari blinked several times. "Oh, yes, c'mon in." She motioned for him to follow her inside.

Grant looked around and was impressed by the warm home Shari had created. The large living room area had a rust-colored sectional sofa, colorful pillows and several interesting sculptures. The walls were filled with pictures of her family and Andre. Andre. Who could be his son!

He'd come to Chicago with a dual purpose of having Lillian's desserts sold at Robinson Restaurants, but also to seek Shari out and see if the passion they'd shared once was still there. But now, everything was different. He could be a father and it was weighing heavy on his heart. He had to know the truth. So tonight was a way for him to spend time with Shari, but it was also a truth-seeking mission to find out if he or Shari's college boyfriend was Andre's father.

Grant swallowed and forced himself to follow Shari as she gave him a short tour of her home. She pointed out the dining room, the master suite with en-suite bathroom and Andre's room, which was painted like a locker room and filled with his toys. They ended the tour in the kitchen with granite countertops and a breakfast nook.

"So what do you think?" Shari asked, turning around to face him. "Not bad for a single mom, huh?"

"Not bad at all," Grant replied. "You have a lovely home."

"Thank you." Shari smiled broadly. "You ready to go?"

Several minutes later, they were seated in his sleek Mercedes Benz with leather interior. "You're driving yourself?" Shari commented when he helped her into the passenger seat before sliding in behind the wheel.

"Yes, does that surprise you?"

"Well, I had heard you'd had a driver earlier."

"He came and got me from O'Hare and took me to my penthouse on Lake Shore Drive where I keep my Benz."

"I didn't realize you had a home in Chicago." It made her nervous to think that Grant had been so close and she hadn't even known it. He could have easily discovered the truth about Andre at any moment.

"Well, I'm in the final stages of acquiring a new restaurant in Lincoln Park, so I thought it would be prudent to have a home here rather than live out of a suitcase."

"Sounds smart, and real estate is always a wise investment. So where are we going?"

"You'll see."

He drove them to Smooth, soon to be the newest Robinson Restaurant in Lincoln Park. Situated along restaurant row near DePaul University, Smooth had the right location to get the young business set and college kids, which kept business steady and created a good income stream.

"You like?" Grant said when they entered the building.

The restaurant was upscale with a wood-paneled ceiling, gleaming tile floors and a carpet inlay. White cushioned booths surrounded the main dining room while oak tables and chairs were in the carpet inlay. A circular bar surrounded the lounge area that had comfy couches and chairs and large televisions mounted to the wall. The lounge doors were opened to let the spring air in.

"It's lovely, Grant," Shari commented. It had an elegant, quiet style that Shari found appealing.

Grant smiled. "Thank you."

The hostess sat them in the private Cellar room made of glass; one wall was filled with various wines from floor to ceiling, and a single table complete with tablecloth, candles and fine china and cutlery awaited them in the center of the room.

"Mr. Robinson, your private waiter Juan will be with you momentarily," the hostess said.

"Thank you," Grant replied, helping Shari into her seat before taking his own.

This was all very fancy, Shari thought to herself, for two friends catching up on old times. Was Grant trying to impress her? If so, he was doing a good job. She rarely got out of the house anymore. Being a single parent precluded her from going out to party like other single women her age. Andre's needs preempted her own and had forced her to grow up pretty quickly.

"You've really outdone yourself," Shari added, glancing around the room.

Grant smiled warmly at the compliment. "I was determined to carve out a place for myself other than what my parents had built. You know, be my own man."

Shari nodded. She understood. It was hard sometimes at Lillian's with so many chiefs who all wanted the spotlight and not enough Indians. It was why sometimes she was content to just fade into the background. It was easier than dealing with all the family drama.

"I remember you mentioning that your parents expected you to take over the family business."

"Yeah, there was a lot of pressure from Pops to settle down."

"You sure did that quick," Shari said, and then realized she spoke out of turn and reached for her water glass to take a sip.

Grant laughed. "Don't be embarrassed. You're right. I got married entirely too quickly. Dina convinced me to have a quickie wedding in Las Vegas a few months after graduating with my MBA from Ledgeman."

Shari wasn't surprised Dina would be in a rush, especially considering she'd probably stolen several Lillian recipes around the same time, so she could open up her own bakery a couple of years later.

"I regretted that marriage almost from the start," Grant continued, "which is why it only lasted less than a year."

"A year?" Shari was shocked. Grant had been single this entire time? *All this wasted time...* But so what? Had she known sooner, would she have done anything differently? Would she really have been able to show up to his doorstep with Andre in tow?

"Yeah, it was a mistake," Grant answered honestly. "Dina and I were cut from the same cloth. Driven and determined to succeed. We didn't mesh well. Everything was always a competition with her, even in our marriage."

Shari wasn't surprised by that statement. She'd come to realize after leaving Ledgeman that she'd been in a competition herself with Dina and hadn't really known it.

The waiter entered the room, introduced himself and

suggested several wines. Grant chose one of his recommendations, which the waiter produced several minutes later. He poured a sip for Grant to taste and after he did, Grant nodded his approval. The waiter filled his glass and poured one for Shari.

After they'd ordered soup for starters and their entrées, Grant turned to Shari. "Enough about me and my failed marriage. I want to hear more about you and what you've been up to the last five years. But first let's toast. To old friends." He raised his wineglass and openly stared at Shari.

Shari found it hard not to be flattered by the attention Grant was bestowing on her. She'd forgotten how good it felt to be with a man. She'd denied herself for too long. "To old friends." She clicked her glass against his. "So what do you want to know?"

"Well, for starters, how about you and Thomas Abernathy?" Grant supplied.

A lump formed in her throat. Shari was surprised Grant even remembered Thomas's name because she'd only mentioned him a few times in passing. "What about him? We hung out in college."

"Well…after you and I were together, after we made love…" Just the words caused a blush to spread across Shari's cheeks. "Well, I thought we might date, but then Dina told me that Thomas was planning to propose to you. That he was an old-fashioned guy and wanted his bride to be a virgin on their wedding night. I felt horrible after our night together, like I'd ruined your plans for your life. But now after seeing Andre…" His voice trailed off.

No wonder Grant felt free to pursue Dina! Dina had

ensured it by spreading lies about her and Thomas. Shari wondered what other lies Dina told him.

"Andre?" Shari swallowed hard. She knew what Grant was implying. He'd assumed like everyone else in the Drayson family that Thomas was Andre's father.

The waiter returned with their soups and Shari sunk her spoon in the creamy mixture and brought it to her lips. The lobster bisque was bright and lush and full of flavor. She didn't like the direction the conversation had turned. She wanted to tell Grant that Andre was his son, but somehow the words wouldn't come. Once he found out, hellfire was sure to rain down on her. She could only imagine how angry he would be with her for keeping the truth from him. Was she being selfish by wanting one more night with him that was just about her and nothing more?

After several moments, she said, "Andre's a great kid. He's smart and funny. He loves to build things and is always asking questions. He's always getting into things. He keeps me on my toes."

"Sounds like a pretty amazing kid," Grant offered.

She tried not to make it obvious that she'd purposely steered the conversation away from Andre's parentage and more into generalities. The subject made her so nervous that she had to fight fidgeting in her seat. Instead, she forced a bright smile.

"He is," she said as she continued eating her soup. "He's the love of my life. Having him was the best decision I ever made."

"How did your family take your pregnancy?"

"They were understandably upset," Shari replied. "They expected me to go to graduate school for my MBA, but it wasn't possible."

"You didn't go?" Grant asked. "Oh, Shari, you were so talented. You had a knack for business."

"Thank you. I appreciate you saying so, but it would have been difficult with a big belly. I didn't want to see the stares of the other students."

"I noticed you haven't mentioned Thomas. Did you go through your pregnancy alone?" Grant circled back to an unwelcome topic.

"Have you met my family?" Shari attempted a laugh even though she felt far from jovial. "I wasn't alone. Eventually, they came around and embraced me and my son."

"I'm so glad. And now you're working at Lillian's?"

"Yes, I'm a baker. You see, we all play a role at Lillian's. My cousin Belinda is tied to Grandma Lillian's apron strings. Belinda keeps the kitchen organized by ordering me, her fiancé, Malik, and my cousin Carter around, even though we're all excellent bakers. Malik, Carter and my cousin Drake are doing a blog called 'Brothers Who Bake,' and now there's talk about a cookbook."

"You sound very impressed with your cousins, but downplay yourself. Why is that?"

It was very intuitive of Grant to feel her ambivalence about her place in the Drayson family.

"With your business degree, you should be running Lillian's."

"I know, I know," Shari said, lowering her head. "And I did by suggesting we sell our bake mixes, which Grandma Lillian implemented. It's just difficult hearing your voice amongst my loud, rambunctious family."

"Then talk louder," Grant offered, and Shari finally chuckled, which helped lighten the mood.

The remainder of the evening was breezy and light with Grant and Shari easily discussing movies, music, cooking and traveling. Shari discovered Grant was well-traveled and had been to Europe, the Middle East and even Africa. She was envious. She'd always wanted to travel, but now that Andre was about to start kindergarten, she was going to be restricted to summer breaks only.

They finished the evening at Chicago's oldest blues club off North Halsted, which was nearly full to capacity. The bar had two stages and two bands. The club was crowded with people lining the walls, drinking at the bar or chowing on their infamous barbecue ribs. Immediately upon entering, Shari noticed the Wall of Fame, which had pictures of the famous blues singers that had sung there. They chose to sit at one of the small, intimate round tables that circled the North Stage.

They listened to some of the best traditional blues Chicago had to offer. The band was great, from the explosive guitar to the sweet sounds of the legendary harmonica. Grant and Shari even got up at one point to share a dance.

She was surprised when Grant suggested it because there were no couples on the floor. Usually Shari hated to be the center of attention, but because Grant was asking, she acquiesced. And she was glad she did.

Being held in Grant's arms was everything she'd dreamed it would be. He was strong, yet gentle as he swayed her to the soft bluesy music. He smelled so manly, earthy and woodsy. She breathed him in, resting her head against his solid chest. At one point, she thought she felt him stroke her shoulder-length hair, but then she realized she was fantasizing too much. Tonight was just about two friends catching up, because surely it couldn't be anything more.

Hours later on the drive to the Drayson family estate at Glenville Heights, they were both introspective, each content with the quiet and the other's presence. Shari had asked Grant to drop her at her parents' home so she could give Andre a kiss good-night and be there when he woke up. Grant hadn't seemed to mind.

When they arrived, the porch light was still on for Shari. She'd called ahead and told her parents she'd be staying over.

Grant turned off the engine and turned and looked at Shari. "I had fun tonight," he said, but didn't move a muscle.

"I did, too," Shari said, wringing her hands in her lap. If this was any other date, she might expect a kiss at the end of the evening, but this was Grant. A man she hadn't seen in years, but with whom she shared a son. What was supposed to happen next? Her anxiety was only increasing because Grant hadn't made a move toward the door. He seemed to be waiting for something, but what?

After several long moments, he said, "I guess we should get you inside."

Shari turned and hazarded a glance in Grant's direction. Desire lurked in those depths, but he seemed to be warring with himself about whether to act on it. She was disappointed when he finally pushed the door open and slid out of the driver's seat. Seconds later, he was opening her door and pulling her out of the car.

Shari used her key to open the front door and turned on the foyer light. That's when she heard the pitter-patter of little feet as her son Andre came bounding down the stairs to her. She bent down and he rushed into her arms. Her little boy had waited up for her.

"Someone should be asleep," she scolded as she lifted her son into her arms.

"I know, Mommy, but you never go away at night," Andre said, "and I couldn't go to sleep. I missed you." He planted a big, sloppy kiss on her cheek.

"I missed you, too," she said, hugging him tightly to her chest, even though she was mortified that Andre had revealed her lack of a love life to Grant. But what could she do? It was already out there. Andre continued chattering on, asking her where she went and what she ate, but Shari barely heard a word because Grant was watching the two of them closely.

She felt so guilty holding Andre. How was she going to tell Grant that Andre was his son? And would he ever forgive her?

Eventually, she lowered Andre to the floor. "You go upstairs to your room." Her parents had made a bedroom especially for their grandson, complete with a Toy Story theme. "And I'll be up in a second to tuck you in. Mommy has to say goodbye to her friend."

She watched Andre pad up the stairs to his room before turning to face Grant. "Thank you for a lovely evening. It was nice getting dressed up. I'd forgotten what it was like."

Grant didn't speak. Instead, he leaned down toward her and Shari's heart caught in her chest. Was he about to kiss her? It was quite the opposite. He looked directly at her and said, "Were you ever planning on telling me?"

Shari was stunned by the change of events. "Excuse me?" She stalled, playing dumb, even though she knew that the truth had caught up to her.

"He's mine, isn't he?" Grant asked, looking up the staircase.

Shari was speechless and didn't…couldn't say a word.

"I don't understand you, Shari. I gave you all night." Grant shook his head in despair. "All night to be honest with me and tell me the truth about Andre. We talked about college and I confided in you about my failed marriage to Dina. I asked you repeatedly about Thomas, but instead, you still said nothing."

Shari finally snapped out of her shock long enough to say, "I'm so sorry, Grant." Her voice broke. "I…I didn't know how to tell you."

Grant took a sharp intake of breath. "You would have continued letting me think that Thomas Abernathy was Andre's father, wouldn't you?"

Shari nervously glanced up the staircase. Now was not the time or the place to talk about this. Not when Andre was within earshot. What if he heard them?

Grant must have realized the exact same thing because he said quietly, "Now is not the right time for this conversation, but trust me, Shari, this is far from over. We will talk in the morning, but know this. Now that I know Andre is my son, I'm not going anywhere."

"I understand." Shari nodded. "And I promise we'll talk in the morning." Her pulse was racing as she ushered him to the door.

"You had better believe it."

Shari took his remark for what it was. A warning.

## Chapter 4

Shari was a nervous wreck as she watched Andre eat his Cocoa Puffs in her parents' kitchen the next morning. Grant knew that Andre was his son and Shari knew hell hath no fury like a father scorned. She could only imagine how upset she'd be if Grant had done the same thing and kept her from Andre. And the truth of the matter was she had no leg to stand on—legal or otherwise. Her only defense was he'd married her former best friend, Dina, and she couldn't handle the betrayal.

Would Grant want shared custody? The thought caused Shari's stomach to churn. She couldn't lose her son. He was her entire world.

Her mother, Lisa Coopersmith Drayson, walked into the kitchen but Shari didn't look up; she was too deep in thought.

"Good morning, baby doll," her mother said as she

bent down and kissed her forehead. "And how's my grandson this morning?"

"Eating Cocoa Puffs." Shari glanced up and looked at her mother. Many would say they looked like sisters because they shared the same big, brown eyes and long, dark hair that went past their shoulders. The only difference was that her mother was dressed fashionably in yoga pants and a sports top.

"Is everything okay?" her mother asked. "You look a little out of sorts this morning. Didn't you sleep well in the guest bedroom?"

"No, I tossed and turned all night," Shari replied. She couldn't sleep because she had no idea what Grant intended to do.

"Well, we heard you get in late last night. Andre here was keeping one eye open and one eye closed," her mother said, ruffling the thick curls on Andre's head. "Must have been some evening. It's not like you to stay out so late."

"It was nice having some male company."

"That Mr. Robinson is quite an attractive young man," her mother commented. "And accomplished, too."

"Really?" Shari looked down and sipped her coffee. She'd made a pot as soon as she'd woken up. Of course, the caffeine only heightened her anxiety. "I hadn't noticed."

"Liar." Her mother laughed and reached across the table for the carafe to pour herself a cup of coffee. "Is he why you're so on edge this morning?"

Shari glanced at her mother. Was she that transparent? "No, why would you say that?"

Her mother smiled knowingly. "Oh, no reason. What are you guys up to today?"

"Well, I was hoping you might be able to watch Andre again for a few hours. I have a quick errand, but I promise I'll be back soon."

"Hmm…another date?" Her mother raised a questioning brow.

Shari ignored the question and rose from her chair. After pouring out her coffee mug and rinsing it out, she bent down and kissed Andre's cheek. "Mommy will be back in a few hours and then we'll go to the park and play. How does that sound?"

"Okay," Andre said and went back to playing with the toy that had come out of the cereal box.

Once she was in her car, Shari allowed herself to take a breath. She had to go to Grant's. No way would she let him come to her territory and risk everyone in the family finding out about her lie of omission. She quickly dialed Carter's number and after getting Grant's address, Shari put the key in the ignition and turned the car on. It was time to face the music.

Grant stared pensively out his penthouse floor-to-ceiling window on Lake Shore Drive and looked out at Lake Michigan. He'd lain in bed for hours staring at the ceiling. By 6:00 a.m., he'd finally given up and gotten out of bed and showered. His mind was a whirl of emotions. He'd come to Chicago to work on his business and maybe even spark up an old flame, but what he'd gotten was much more than he bargained for. He was a father. He had a son.

Despite Shari finally admitting the truth, Grant had known the moment he'd set eyes on Andre at Lillian's that the little boy was his. He had his green eyes, dimples and fair coloring. It was like looking at a mini-me.

But was he even ready to be a father? Shari had pregnancy and four years to prepare for the role, but Grant? He'd just been thrown into fatherhood with no preamble and certainly no thanks to Shari. She would probably have kept Grant in the dark if he hadn't made this trip to Chicago. He didn't know whether to strangle her or kiss those big, brown lips of hers senseless.

Although fatherhood was a role he hadn't wanted for a few years yet, now that it was in his lap, he intended to do right by his son.

A knock on his penthouse door roused Grant out of his daze and back to reality. Before he opened the door, he knew who would be standing on the other side. No one knew where he was staying or would have any reason to visit him this early in the morning. It had to be Shari.

He opened the door and found her staring up at him. Her long, black hair had been pulled into a simple ponytail and she was wearing a black-and-white-trimmed tunic and white jeans.

"May I come in?" she asked when he stared at her, motionless.

He didn't speak; instead, he stepped aside, allowing her to enter the penthouse.

Shari didn't take a moment to absorb his expensive furniture or his posh surroundings; she just started firing on attack mode. "Listen, I know you're upset with me," she began, pacing the ceramic tile floor, "and you have every right to be, but I would like the chance to explain."

Grant followed silently behind her and motioned for

her to sit on the couch as he plopped down in a leather chair adjacent to her. He folded his arms across his chest, eager to see what spin she could put on the fact that she'd kept his son from him for four years.

"Umm…where do I begin?" Shari said, sitting down and tossing her purse on the coffee table. "Okay, I guess I'll start at the beginning."

"That would be good."

Shari rolled her eyes at his sarcasm, but maintained her composure. "I found out I was pregnant soon after our night together at Ledgeman. I wanted to tell you." When she noticed Grant's raised eyebrow, she pressed, "I did. I even tried to tell you, but then I saw you and Dina holding hands in the courtyard and my heart sank."

Shari glanced up at him, but Grant didn't say a word. He wanted her to get whatever she needed to off her chest before he told her how he felt.

"I know it's my fault. I mean, I did tell you that our night together was just a hookup. And I said that because I didn't want you to feel like you owed me anything seeing as how it was my first time."

Grant sat upright in his chair. He hadn't realized she'd been a virgin when they'd slept together. He could have done so much better by her if she'd given him the opportunity, and this information only made him angrier.

"Anyway, how could I have known that I'd end up pregnant after one night?" She attempted a laugh but it sounded shrill to Grant. "And then right before summer break, I heard that you were engaged and I was hurt. And maybe subconsciously, I kept the truth as a way to hurt you and Dina. I admit that, but I just couldn't bear the thought of her helping to raise my child. And…"

Grant held up his hand. "Let me ask you one question. Would you ever have told me the truth if I hadn't come to Chicago?"

Tears formed in Shari's eyes and she looked away, unable to meet his gaze.

"I thought so," Grant responded, rising to his feet. "You would have continued to leave me and my son in the dark."

"Oh, God!" Shari's hand went to her mouth. Hearing the words made her sound so cold, so heartless, but that was never her intention. Her heart had just been broken. "Grant…"

"I lost four years of Andre's life." Grant glared at her with reproachful eyes. "Years I can't get back! But you can best believe that I don't plan on missing one more minute of my son's life."

"You can have as much access to Andre as you like," Shari said as she sniffed. She reached for her purse and withdrew a tissue to blow her nose. "I wouldn't keep him from you. I promise. We can come up with a visitation schedule that's fair and equitable to the both of us."

"Not good enough," Grant stated. "I won't be a part-time father, not after the time I've lost."

He saw the dread fill Shari at his words. "Do…do you intend on seeking full custody?"

"I won't have to because we're getting married," Grant returned in a cool, aloof manner. "Tomorrow."

"What did you just say?"

"You heard right."

"That's crazy!" Shari sputtered. "We don't even know each other."

"No crazier than having a baby and neglecting to tell the father," Grant responded, affronted by her tone.

Shari shook her head. "No, no, this is lunacy. Marriage isn't necessary," she continued. "We're smart people, Grant. We can figure this out, so neither one of us feels slighted. You just need time to calm down and when you do, we can talk about this like adults." She rose and reached for her purse on the coffee table, but Grant reached out and clasped her arm, preventing her from going.

"It's been settled. We are getting married."

"Or else what?" Shari asked defiantly, snatching her arm away. She lifted her chin and boldly met his angry gaze.

Grant shot her a penetrating look, his vexation with her evident. "Or else I petition for full custody of Andre."

"You wouldn't do that!" Shari gasped. "You wouldn't take a son from his mother. I'm all he's ever known…" Her voice began to tremble. "You…you saw for yourself. Andre is a happy, well-adjusted child. He's had a life filled with love from me and my family."

"But not from me." Grant saw the fear, stark and vivid in Shari's eyes. He was bluffing about suing for custody, but he would never let Shari know that. "Listen, Shari. There's no reason this has to turn ugly." His tone turned soft. "You must see that raising Andre in a two-parent home is the best way. Think about the life we could give him."

"A life with parents who don't love each other?" Shari asked incredulously.

Grant was surprised by her candor and didn't answer her question. He knew what it was like to grow up with parents in a loveless marriage, and he didn't want that for Andre. Somehow, he would find a way to make a marriage with Shari work. At the heart of it, he was at the very least attracted to her. But he didn't say that. Instead he said, "You've done a good job raising Andre until now, Shari. I don't diminish that. But our son would finally have a father, and he'd finally be legitimate and not a bastard!"

"Ouch!" Shari turned away as emotions crossed her face. Was one of them guilt? Grant knew he was hitting below the belt to convince her to marry him.

He knew he'd been brutal, but he had to be. He didn't want Shari to test him because if she did, he would buckle. He would never take Andre from her, yet he wanted a stable home for his son. "Those are my terms. Take it or leave it."

Shari shrugged with resignation and replied in a low, tormented voice, "Okay."

Grant walked toward her and lifted her chin. "What was that?" His gaze traveled over her face and searched her big, brown eyes.

Shari looked up at him, and Grant felt the blood rush through him. "I said I will marry you."

"Then let's kiss on it." Before Grant knew what he was doing, he was lowering his head and slowly brushing his lips across Shari's. He hadn't meant to kiss her. He was still furious and wanted to throttle her, but she'd looked so vulnerable, like she had that night so many years ago, that again he was powerless to resist.

Her lips were soft and moist and she tasted as sweet as he remembered that night in the dorm. Grant lost himself in the kiss and circled his arm around her waist, pulling her closer to him. He deepened the kiss by using his tongue to trace the outline of her lips until she parted her mouth and opened up to him. He wrapped his tongue around hers, entwining it with his, sucking it, devouring it. Shari didn't object. She responded to his kiss.

The ringing of a cell phone snapped Grant out of the kiss just as if someone had poured cold water over him. What was he doing? He was kissing the woman who'd kept his son a secret from him for four years.

Roughly, he pushed Shari away from him and walked away to the window. Why the hell had he kissed her? Maybe because he'd secretly been wanting to do that from the moment he laid eyes on her again? He'd wanted to taste her sweetness and see if she tasted as good as he remembered.

He heard Shari from behind him on the phone. "Oh, yes, of course. I'd forgotten about the birthday party. Yes, I'll bring Andre and we'll be there shortly." Inhaling, Grant took a deep breath and then turned back around.

Shari looked dazed as if she'd been thoroughly kissed and she had, but the words that came out of her mouth were far from sweet. "If you insist on this farce of a marriage, then fine. But it will not be tomorrow. I will not have some quickie marriage like you did with Dina just because you say so. I have a family and we have a son and he deserves a wedding since we're doing this for him."

Grant nodded in agreement. Shari had a point. "You're right. We should have a proper ceremony. A week or two should be enough time for us to put together a small wedding."

"Fine. Since this is your suggestion, why don't you

let me know where and when and then I'll just show up," she replied cattily. "I have to go." She swung the purse over her shoulder and seconds later she was out the door.

Grant sighed as he watched the door close. He'd gotten what he wanted. Now what?

Once she was in her car, Shari burst into tears. She was finally going to marry the man of her dreams, Grant Robinson. In a fairy-tale world, Grant would profess his undying love to her and tell her he'd never stopped thinking about her. He would tell her he'd come back to Chicago *for her.* But he wasn't saying that. He was offering a marriage of convenience for their son. Grant didn't want her, probably never had. The only reason he'd kissed her just now was because they were stuck with each other. He probably was preparing himself for the fact that he'd be shackled to her for the rest of his life and had better start enjoying the prospect.

How had everything changed so suddenly? She'd been so sure this morning that she could convince Grant to see reason and they could come to some sort of custody arrangement. But he'd been unwilling to give an inch. Marriage or risk losing custody of her son. Grant could be bluffing about taking her to court, but she wasn't prepared to put her son's future on the line.

Grant had given logical reasons why marriage could be beneficial for them both, but none of those reasons included love. And despite the past five years and even his behavior now, she still loved Grant. She probably always would. The only bright spot in his rushing her to the altar was that in a few weeks she would come face-to-face with her nemesis and Grant's ex-wife, Dina English. Except this time, she'd be the one with Grant's wedding ring on her finger where it should have been since college. Had he known she was carrying Andre, would he have married her, instead? Shari would never know because she'd been too afraid to tell him.

## Chapter 5

Shari worried about telling her family about her wedding to Grant and that he was Andre's father. It would come as a shock to them. They'd all assumed that poor Thomas was the culprit. And worse yet, how was she going to tell Andre? She needn't have worried because she was in for a shock when her cousin Belinda called her the following morning.

"Okay, what gives?" Belinda asked on the other end of the line.

"What are you talking about?"

"You called a family meeting at Grandma Lillian's, at the estate," Belinda replied. "No, make that Grant Robinson called a meeting for noon."

"He did what?" Shari tried to interrupt, but her cousin was still ranting. Grant was making a preemptive strike. He wanted her family on his side. Once the Draysons found out Grant was Andre's father, they would push the union. It was ingenious, if Shari believed he wanted to marry her, but she knew otherwise.

"Who the hell does he think he is? He doesn't even know us. Just because Uncle Dwight is singing his praises about Lillian's and Robinson Restaurants having a joint venture doesn't mean—"

"He's my fiancé," Shari stated, interrupting her cousin's rant.

All conversation halted and Shari could have sworn Belinda dropped the phone because she heard a lot of shuffling before her cousin returned to the phone and asked. "Did you say *fiancé?*"

Shari sighed. She might as well get it out of the way and deal with some of the histrionics now. "I'm getting married." She tried to sound happy.

"What? You haven't even mentioned the man in years since college and now I'm supposed to believe that you're an item, let alone about to get married? Are you trying to punk me?"

"No. And I really have no time to waste or I'll be late to the meeting," Shari said. "But I'll see you soon." She hung up the line as soon as she could. She wasn't prepared to give an explanation because she'd been completely taken off guard. Clearly sleeping on it had done no good because Grant was ready to proceed as planned, and he was enlisting her family to finish strong-arming her to the altar.

When she arrived at the Drayson estate in Glenville Heights, the majority of the family was already there. Shari tried to postpone the inevitable for as long as she could by staying in the car. When the clock struck noon, she finally exited her vehicle.

She'd let Andre play at a friend's house in the hopes that she would find the words to tell him that his father was alive and well. She'd never told Andre his father was dead, just that he wasn't a part of their lives, but she knew that's what he thought. It was going to come as a shock when she did tell him the truth.

"Congratulations, baby girl." Her father came forward and pulled his eldest child into a warm hug as soon as she entered the living room.

Her eyes immediately connected with Grant's green ones from across the room. He was making sure that if she had any doubts about backing out of their deal, he wasn't having it. "I'm so sorry, my darling," Grant said, walking toward her, "but I just couldn't resist spilling the beans."

When he reached her, he leaned down. "Where have you been?" he asked. "And where's Andre?"

Shari was momentarily struck by how handsome Grant was in his dress trousers and navy silk shirt. The shirt was unbuttoned at the nape and Shari knew what lay underneath because she'd felt his hard muscular body when he'd kissed her at his penthouse.

"At a friend's," Shari whispered breathlessly. Clearly, his loving and affectionate tone was only for her family's benefit.

"Even now you're trying to keep me from him," Grant said, so that she alone could hear.

Shari smiled blandly since everyone in the family was watching their interaction. "I wanted to keep him out of this charade for as long as possible."

"My son doesn't need protection from me."

Shari didn't get to answer because Carter came toward them. "You sure know how to keep things under wraps, cuz," he said, hugging her warmly. "I knew you two knew each other, but marriage?"

"It's a shock." Belinda was instantly at Carter's side. Her eyes were sharp and assessing as she tried to read Shari's expression and body language.

"Not really," Grant replied. "When you consider how long Shari and I have known each other. And given that we share a son." He said the words loud enough for everyone to hear. "I think our marriage is long overdue."

Boom. Grant had dropped the bombshell. Shari sucked in a breath and waited for all hell to break loose in her family.

"What?" Her mother looked at her imploringly from the couch. "Shari, what is he talking about?"

"I knew it!" Carter snapped his fingers. "I knew Andre looked like you," he told Grant.

Shari felt all eyes in the room on her at once. She glanced around and saw Grandma Lillian staring at her with sad eyes. She'd lied to them all. Of course, she hadn't seen it that way. She'd actually never told them Thomas was the father. They'd just assumed he was and she'd let them.

Shari glanced up at Grant and he shrugged. He was going to let her ride this rough patch out on her own. She cleared her throat before saying, "Grant is Andre's father."

"How long have you known?" her father asked. "How long have you kept the truth from us?"

The hurt and betrayal she heard in her father's voice pulled at Shari's heartstrings and made her feel terrible. Her eyes began to water and a stray tear fell to her cheek, which she wiped away with the back of her hand. "I…I've always known."

"But you allowed us to condemn Thomas, an innocent man," her uncle Devon said harshly. "Typical woman!" he snorted.

Shari wasn't surprised by his comment. Her uncle had always had an aversion to committing to a woman, let alone marrying one. He'd never married Carter's mother, Marion Daniels, which was probably why Carter always felt like an outcast in the family.

"And you?" her father asked Grant. "How long have you known?"

"Does it really matter?" Shari asked. She didn't want to get into the particulars of her past with her entire family. "Suffice it to say that once I told Grant, the connection we shared since before Dina came into the picture, resurfaced."

The name caused commotion in the room and had the desired effect. Her family was more concerned with Dina and less about when Grant knew the truth.

"And now we're just two long-lost lovebirds reconnecting, and we don't want to waste another minute. And we want to become a family for Andre," Shari said, circling her arms around Grant's waist. "Isn't that right, sweetie?" She looked up at him and gave him a loving smile.

Grant took the bait and went along. "I admit, it was difficult finding out about a son I never knew, but Shari is so special to me." He tucked a wayward strand of hair out of her face and then bent to brush his lips across hers. "I couldn't bear to let her go again." He kissed her and despite it all, Shari felt her inner resistance surrender. No, she told herself, it was simply a convincing performance.

"This is so surreal," her sister Monica said from

across the room. Shari had never confided in her about having had a crush on Grant back in college. In fact, she'd always kept mum when it came to talking about Andre's father.

"Has anyone told Andre?" her mother asked.

Shari shook her head.

"But we will," Grant answered immediately. "I want him to be a part of the wedding in a couple of weeks."

"Excuse me?" her mother replied. "Did you say a couple of weeks?"

"Yes, ma'am." Grant nodded and pulled Shari closer. She knew he had to make their sudden marriage believable to her family. "We don't want to wait."

"Why the rush?" Grandma Lillian finally spoke up.

Shari was surprised she'd been quiet this long. The family matriarch wasn't known for being bashful.

Grant was quick to answer—a little too quick for Shari's liking—and said, "Well, Shari and I haven't been able to keep our hands off each other..." He let the words dangle in the air.

Shari blushed a thousand shades of red. Grant's implication was they'd been intimate again and the chance of another Andre was possible.

"Well, I for one think it's great that you're going to make an honest woman out of my daughter," Dwight replied and came forward to shake Grant's hand. "Given the circumstances."

"I don't know," Grandma Lillian said with a stern expression. "This is all moving so fast. How is my great-grandson going to handle a new father and the two of you getting married? It might be too much."

"Or it might be exactly what my son needs," Grant countered in a respectful tone. "Stability."

Grandma Lillian was silent. It was one of the few times that someone spoke up to her. Shari liked that Grant wasn't afraid to his speak his mind.

"Well, if this is going to happen," her mother said, "then what can we do? There's not much time to put together a wedding."

Shari turned to Grant. She'd told him to tell her where and when and she'd show up. She hadn't considered her family might want to play a role.

Before she knew it, she was sitting down in the kitchen with her mother, Monica, Aunt Daisy and Belinda discussing wedding plans.

"Of course, the cake has to be made by Lillian's," Grandma Lillian said, joining them in the kitchen with her book of cake ideas. Shari could tell she was more than hesitant about their marrying, but despite her reservations, she was ready to pitch in. They all began flipping through her grandmother's book. Meanwhile, the menfolk were in the living room discussing venues, DJ and the photographer. All except her uncle Devon who had departed, wanting no part of the rushed nuptials.

"This is all so sudden," her mother said, reaching across and grabbing Shari's hand. "I mean, I've barely had time to digest that Grant is Andre's father, let alone that you're getting married in a couple of weeks."

"Well, we love each other," Shari added. She had to continue to spin the web of lies, otherwise her family would never believe this sudden union.

"But you never talked about him," her sister Monica said from across the table.

"Not to you," Belinda responded.

"What do you mean?" Grandma Lillian immediately zeroed in on her favorite grandchild.

"I remember Shari mentioning Grant while they were in college," Belinda said. "She used to gush about him to me and Dina."

"Don't speak that woman's name in this house," Shari hissed.

Belinda held up her hands. "Sorry. I'm just saying that you were crazy about Grant back then, but I wasn't sure your feelings were reciprocated."

"Well, clearly they were," Shari replied harshly. "Or I wouldn't have conceived Andre."

"I know. I'm just surprised that you're getting married before me," Belinda replied huffily.

"All right, all right," Grandma Lillian said. "No need to bicker. Andre is the light of our lives and we are happy to have Grant join our family if that's what you truly want." Her grandmother gave Shari a truth-beseeching look.

Shari wanted to tell her grandmother the truth that although she loved Grant, the feeling was not mutual, but she couldn't. "Of course it's what I want." She plastered a smile on her face. "Grant is everything I've ever wanted."

"Then you're going to need a dress," her mother said, which made Aunt Daisy jump up to find a measuring tape. "And we don't have much time."

Shari sat at the kitchen table in a bewildered state as the women in her family shuffled around her.

Grant had to despise her for keeping the truth about Andre from him. Even though she knew logically that children fared better in a two-parent household, she couldn't figure out for the life of her why Grant would want to shackle himself to her for the rest of his life. Or maybe he was using this marriage as a tactic. Maybe to

show she was an unfit mother so he could eventually
sue for custody. Or perhaps she was overthinking it,
and he truly wanted to do right by Andre. Shari didn't
know what to believe or what to expect from Grant out
of this marriage.

Grant was unprepared for the onslaught of the Drayson family when they put their minds to something.
Once he'd said they were getting married in a couple of
weeks, the Drayson clan sprang into action. The thought
about planning the wedding himself quickly went out
the window.

The men had decided to take a divide and conquer
approach and had divvied up the tasks. Shari's father
had quickly called their pastor, who'd agreed to perform
the ceremony in the family's church. Carter was calling
a DJ friend that he knew, while Drake, thanks to his
marketing connections, was lining up a videographer.

He'd recalled back in the day that Shari said her
family was a force of nature. Now he was seeing them
in action. While the men were on the phone haggling,
Grant took a moment to step away. He left the living
room and strolled through the family estate. He wanted,
no *needed* to find Shari to make sure she wasn't about
to renege on their agreement. He'd sprung this marriage thing on her and then reinforced it by beating her
to the punch and telling her family. Given the speed
of the situation, she could be having second thoughts.

He found her with the rest of the Drayson women
sitting at the kitchen table, which was covered with
wedding books. Apparently, Belinda and Carter were
both on the marriage track so the family had them read-
ily available. Grant watched Shari from the doorway.
She sat quietly listening as the rest of her family was

bustling about her. That's what he remembered about Shari in college, the quiet ease he'd felt whenever he was around her.

Was that why he'd behaved rashly? When she'd come over to his penthouse after he'd confronted her with the truth, he certainly hadn't planned on proposing marriage. But when she'd been so logical and reasonable about sharing custody after keeping his son from him, something in him just snapped. He'd refused to be swept under the rug as if his feelings weren't important. He deserved a place in Andre's life and would not be a "see you on the weekend" kind of father.

The marriage idea had sprung in his head and he'd acted on it impulsively. The more Shari dug her heels in, the more he wanted it. Why was she acting as if the idea was so repugnant to her, when he knew for a fact that at the very least she still desired him? He'd known that night after taking her to his restaurant that she'd wanted him. He'd felt her nipples pucker underneath the flimsy material of the dress she was wearing. And she'd certainly responded to his kiss to seal the deal at his penthouse. As had he.

Where was all this lust coming from now? He'd always wanted her, but he could never have predicted she'd been holding on to such a monumental secret. He was livid with her, and his mind told him to keep their marriage one of convenience—for the time being, anyway. But then again, his body yearned to taste her again, to feel her against him. Just how long would he be able to hold out from taking his soon-to-be wife to bed?

As if she sensed him, Shari raised her eyes to find Grant watching her from the doorway. The women in her family were so preoccupied that they barely noticed her scooting out of her chair and leaving the room.

"Can we talk?" Grant asked in a low and smooth voice. "Privately."

"Let's go outside," Shari said.

Grant followed her out the side entrance into a beautifully landscaped garden.

Once they'd gone a safe distance, she turned to face him. "What's so important? Do you have something else to blindside me with?" she asked curtly, folding her arms across her chest. She didn't appreciate his sucker punch in telling her family about their marriage.

Grant looked shocked by her haughty attitude. "Are you serious? You're the one that kept my son away from me."

"And you're the one who's forcing me into marrying you."

"I don't see any shackles around you." Grant's lips thinned with irritation as he looked down at her delicate wrists. "You're free to do as you like. Because for some, marrying me wouldn't be that bad of a prospect."

"Not without consequences," Shari retorted.

"Ah, yes." Grant walked toward her until he was inches away from her. "That nasty little thing called consequences. But let's not forget why we're here, Shari. We're here because you couldn't be honest with me."

"I know, Grant, I know." Shari threw her arms up in self-defense. "What I did was wrong, but what you're doing is no better."

"I'm doing what's best for my son."

"My son," Shari countered.

Grant glared at her, frowning. "*Our* son."

His statement caused Shari to sigh heavily and she

lowered her head. For four years, she'd only thought of Andre as her son. Though she knew he and Grant shared DNA, she'd buried it in the dark recesses of her mind, and now he was forcing her to deal with the cold, hard truth. Decisions regarding Andre were not hers alone to make anymore.

When she looked back up, tears were shimmering in her eyes. One fell down her cheek and Grant reached and caught the teardrop with his thumb. Why was he trying to be kind now? It made Shari feel even worse. "I'm sorry, okay? I don't know what more I can say. I've agreed to fix this by marrying you. Isn't that enough?"

"So you won't back out?" Grant asked.

Shari shook her head.

"Good," Grant said. "Since its official, you'd better wear this." He fished in his pants pocket and produced a black box.

Shari had no time to react because Grant was sliding a platinum, six-carat diamond engagement ring on her left hand. An emerald-cut diamond was in the center with small diamonds encrusted on the band. The ring felt cool between her fingers, but she felt warm because having Grant's hands on her caused a jolt of awareness to shoot through her.

He was staring at her again with those stunning green eyes of his, and Shari felt like he wanted to kiss her again like he'd done in his penthouse, but this time he didn't. Grant stepped away from her.

"Now the women in your family will have something to gush over."

Shari swallowed, trying to remove the lump in her throat, but it seemed permanently lodged there whenever Grant was around.

Shari held up her hand and admired the diamond. "It's beautiful. How did you get it so fast?"

"I have my ways," Grant replied. "Get used to it because things are about to change once you become Mrs. Robinson."

That's exactly what Shari was afraid of.

## Chapter 6

The two weeks before their marriage went by in a blur, except for the moment when she and Grant sat down with Andre and told him Grant was his father.

She'd never seen such joy in her son at finally being able to see himself in another man. She hadn't known Andre had been wanting, missing and needing a father until he'd rushed into Grant's embrace, accepting him with open arms. All this time, she'd thought she'd been enough. How wrong she'd been! A tiny piece of her heart broke because she could have given Andre a father much sooner if it hadn't been for her stupid pride.

The love that was etched across Grant's face at holding Andre in his arms was indescribable. Shari doubted she'd ever forget it. It was as if he'd come home. And so, she rose from the couch to leave the room to give father and son their privacy.

"Thank you," Grant mouthed to her as she left.

Nearly half an hour later, Grant and Andre found her in the kitchen and asked her to go a Cubs game. Grant had scored three tickets next to the dugout. Andre was so excited; he was jumping up and down.

"Mommy, Mommy, can we go, pretty please?" Andre inquired.

"Are you sure you want me to go?" Shari asked Andre, but looked at Grant as she asked the question. "I mean, I don't want to intrude on your bonding time."

"And you're not. We want you to come," Grant said, his green eyes never leaving her face. "It's why I bought three tickets."

"You have to come," Andre said. He grabbed her hand first and then Grant's. "We can go to the game as a family with a mommy *and* a daddy."

Tears welled in Shari's eyes. Grant had been right. Marrying him was the right thing to do for Andre. She swallowed. "All right." Her mouth spread into a smile. "I'd like that very much."

If anyone had told Shari a week ago that she would be sharing hot dogs, popcorn and soda with Andre and Grant, her soon-to-be husband, she would have called them a liar. Never in her wildest dreams would she have imagined that one day they would spend time together as a family, but that was exactly what they did. They watched the game and Grant clapped when he liked a play or shouted at the umpire when he didn't. Andre mimicked everything that Grant did and Shari couldn't help laughing at just how much the two resembled each other, especially when Grant bought himself and Andre matching Cubs jerseys.

When the game was over, Andre grasped Shari's hand in one hand and Grant's in the other as they walked down the breezeway to leave. Shari looked at Grant and gave him a wink and they swung Andre up in the air. Andre laughed and hooted and hollered. It was the happiest Shari had ever seen him and she was delighted.

Once they made it back to her house, Andre was exhausted and the poor thing went down for a nap leaving Grant and Shari alone. *Now what?* she wondered.

"Today was really great," Shari said, attempting to make light conversation as they stood awkwardly outside Andre's bedroom door in the hall.

Grant smiled and it reached his eyes. "Yeah, it was. Andre's a great kid. You've done a fantastic job raising him, Shari."

"Thank you. That means a lot coming from you," Shari replied.

"So…you see how good it could be?"

Shari glanced up at him and she got the distinct impression that Grant was not merely talking about his relationship with Andre, but about their becoming a family. "Yes" was all she could mutter before Grant's large hands reached for her and his body backed her up against the wall.

He sealed his mouth on hers before she had a chance to object and then he teased the seam of her closed lips until she parted them, allowing him to thrust his tongue in her mouth. His kiss was soft, then urgent and reckless, eroding the delicate balance she was holding on to. It reminded Shari of a passion she'd long since forgotten and hadn't had with a man since…well, since Grant. A ribbon of desire coiled inside her and Shari knew she wanted him, and the knowledge that she needed to be with him both excited and scared her.

As the lip-lock went on, Shari moved against his unyielding weight, letting out a low moan of appreciation when his hips settled between her thighs. When his body pressed against hers, she felt his hard erection throbbing against her soft body and it sent heat jolting through her. Grant was hard *everywhere*.

"Where's your bedroom?" he barked out.

Shari inclined her head, and Grant backed her down the hall and pushed the door to her bedroom open with his foot. Next thing Shari knew he was pushing her down onto her queen-size bed and sliding on top of her. He thrust his hands into her hair and seconds later brought his lips down on hers. Deepening the kiss, he thrust his slippery-as-silk tongue in and out of her mouth again mimicking lovemaking. It was a long and indecent kiss, but Shari reveled in his insistent exploration, tasting him and drinking him in.

Grant wasn't just kissing her; his hands were roaming over her entire body. He stopped at her breasts, molding and shaping the rounded mounds of flesh with his hands. Her nipples puckered tightly underneath the cotton shirt she wore when the pads of Grant's thumbs teased the buds. She so desperately wanted him to remove the confinement of her bra and take them in his mouth.

Her breath hitched when he wound his hips in circles against her. She arched her body toward him and shamelessly grinded against him. And Grant, as if understanding her reflexive response, gave it to her. Harder, then faster. Shari moaned and that only seemed to make Grant move quicker. He pumped his hips into hers.

Harder. Faster. Shari trembled, twitched and let out a scream. Grant covered her mouth with his, absorbing her moans so as to not wake up Andre.

When the tremors subsided, Shari was embarrassed at how loud she'd been, but apparently not nearly as embarrassed as Grant because he suddenly tore away from her and sat on the edge of her bed.

Grant hadn't meant for things to get out of control so quickly, but when she began moaning, he'd wanted to give her the pleasure and orgasm she so desperately needed. And now? He wanted more than anything to strip her naked and make love to her until she couldn't remember her name. He wanted every part of her body and there was no mistaking that she wanted him. But they had a lot of history between them, a lot of hurt and anger that, although he desired her, he wasn't sure they could overcome.

He hoped in the future he would be able to look at Shari and not remember that she'd kept his son away from him, but instead look back at what a happy life they shared together. Unfortunately, today was not that day.

"This isn't going to happen," Grant said, backpedaling out of an awkward situation. He'd gotten Shari all worked up and he knew she had to be wet for him, ready for him, but he just couldn't go there.

"Clearly," she responded, grasping a nearby pillow and holding it tightly against her chest. "Do you get a kick out of tripping me up, Grant, and playing this cat-and-mouse game? You want me, but then you don't? Is this your way of making me pay for keeping Andre away from you?"

"Of course not," Grant replied as if offended by her words. "I never meant for that to happen."

"No?" Shari said, her anger starting to rise. She jumped to her feet. "Fine, then just go." She was humiliated by her wanton body's reaction to him.

"Shari…" Grant stood up.

"I said go," Shari replied. "I want to be alone."

Grant hated to leave on these terms, especially after they'd enjoyed such a great day. "Okay, I'll go, but I'll call you later."

Once he got in his Mercedes Benz, Grant sighed heavily. Shari was sexy as hell and he was attracted to the beautiful baker who was going to be his wife in a few short days. But he was imposing celibacy on himself to keep the minx from capturing his heart.

What the hell was he going to do?


"You look stunning, baby girl," Dwight Drayson told Shari at the end of the week as they stood in the vestibule of the family church in Glendale Heights waiting for their cue. Her wedding party—Drake and Monica, Belinda and Malik, Carter and his fiancée, Lorraine—had already walked down the aisle.

"Thank you, Daddy," Shari said as she looked down the aisle and saw Grant waiting with the minister at the end.

When Shari had asked Grant about his parents or inviting other family members, he'd adamantly refused. He'd told her his parents were on a cruise to the Mexican Riviera, but he'd indicated he would tell them afterward. Shari wasn't sure how to feel about the fact that Grant wasn't introducing her and Andre to his family, but it was his decision.

The "Wedding March" sounded and her father turned to her. "You ready to go?"

After taking several deep breaths to compose herself, Shari nodded. She walked down the aisle toward Grant in a daze. She was about to say her vows to her first love, the man with whom she shared an adoring son, who was smiling at her from his father's side, wearing a miniature tuxedo and holding the ring pillow.

Shari was scared to death.

Was she making a mistake by aligning herself to Grant for the rest of her life? Of course, there was always divorce, but she didn't believe in divorce. Marriage was for keeps. And so as she walked down the aisle, Shari vowed to do everything in her power to make the marriage work. *Please God, please make Grant fall in love with me,* she prayed. *Let this marriage work. Make us become a real family.*

Their honeymoon would be the start. Grant was attracted to her; that much she knew. He'd had a raging hard-on the last time they were together at her house, something he was trying to keep in check, but for how long? He wouldn't be able to deny his body's needs for too long. He would have to give in.

Shari and her father made it to the end of the aisle. Her father extended her hand to Grant and whispered, "Take care of my daughter."

"I will, sir," Grant said.

Shari and Grant exchanged vows with her entire family in attendance. The wedding, although small, was exquisite. Grant had thought of everything, from the beautiful flowers that adorned the pews to the white rose and oriental lily bouquet in her hand to the fitted white trumpet gown with floral appliqué and lace that she wore. The Drayson women had gushed when they saw Shari in the fitted dress, and so had Shari. After wearing nothing but jeans and T-shirts for years, she felt beautiful in the exquisite gown.

When it was time to kiss the bride, Shari wasn't sure what Grant was going to do, but he didn't disappoint. He kissed her as he'd done that day in his penthouse, except a bit more chastely because her family was around.

They jumped the broom and the minister announced they were husband and wife. "I introduce you to Mr. and Mrs. Grant Robinson," he said, amongst cheers and applause from her family in the pews.

"It's time to cut the cake," Shari's mother said after dinner had been served and several speeches had been made. Shari was touched when her father and Carter got up to wish them the best.

It made Shari feel terrible that she was deceiving them and letting them believe she and Grant had a real marriage when in reality it was a farce.

But Shari put on a happy face, anyway, because her family was so proud of the wedding cake they'd created for her special day. It was a three-tier chocolate cake with strawberry filling, complete with a cascade of fresh flowers that matched her bouquet.

Shari joined Grant in the center of the room as a waiter wheeled the decadent cake in front of them. She reached for the spatula and then turned to Grant. "Do not smush cake in my face," she warned.

"Who, me?" He winked at her devilishly as he set his large hand over hers so they could cut a slice of cake together. Once cut, Shari placed a sliver of cake on a plate and as was custom, they both fingered a piece off and fed each other. When Grant licked the icing off her fingers, a shot of electricity went right through Shari.

Grant looked like he wanted to devour her, but just as quickly, the look was gone.

Her mother stepped in and began cutting cake for the rest of the wedding party, while Shari went to find her son. She needed a breather from the sexual tension sizzling between her and Grant, otherwise she would combust.

Grant watched Shari voraciously from across the room as she danced with their son. She'd lifted Andre in her arms and was circling the floor with him. She'd been the most beautiful bride as she'd walked down the aisle toward him. The dress he'd chosen for her fit her curvy figure like a glove. In that moment, his heart welled with a foreign emotion. He wasn't sure it was love, but maybe affection?

The weeks before the wedding, they'd been pretty much attached at the hip except during the day when she was working in the bakery and he was checking in on his restaurants. Thanks to Andre and Shari, his whole life was about to change.

Although he had a new restaurant in Chicago and owned a penthouse here, he'd been based primarily in New York because he'd loved the bustling lights of the city, but his son's life was here. He couldn't uproot Andre and take him away from his family when he was already getting a father he'd never met. Not to mention, he doubted Shari would leave Lillian's. She'd confided in him that her grandmother was soon to retire and would leave the running of Lillian's most likely to one of her grandchildren. And it could be Shari.

Grant knew Shari was quite capable of running Lillian's. She was not only beautiful, but smart. She had a knack for figures and business. He'd seen it when he'd taken graduate-level classes with her at Ledgeman.

He was surprised how in a short amount of time, Shari had gotten under his skin. After their night together five years ago, he'd always wondered if there could have been more between the two of them if Dina hadn't come into the picture. He'd been blinded by Dina's charm and her aggressiveness. Dina was a real go-getter and wouldn't take no for an answer. She'd hounded him relentlessly until he'd finally agreed to date her, even though he'd held a torch for her roommate.

Why hadn't Shari shared with him that she was carrying his child? Who knows what life they could have had together if only she'd told him she was pregnant. Now he'd lost precious years with Andre that he could never get back, and clearly Andre had yearned for a father. The way he'd hugged Grant when they'd told him the truth had struck a chord with him that would never be broken. He vowed at that moment to spend the rest of his life making it up to his son. But his anger at Shari was also why even though he desired her and wanted her in his bed tonight, he wouldn't come to her. He didn't trust her.

"You all right?" Carter asked when he came to stand beside Grant.

Grant glanced at Carter. "Yeah, man. I'm okay."

"She looks beautiful, doesn't she?" Carter said, watching Shari and Andre on the dance floor.

Grant smiled. "She's wearing the hell out of that

dress." He'd known she would look good in it when he'd selected it.

"I hear you," Carter said. "I know Lorraine will look equally as good at our wedding. Of course, unlike you, we are not rushing to the altar. Lorraine and her family want a big, traditional wedding."

"We didn't rush," Grant said, looking at Shari intently. "This marriage was inevitable."

"After one fateful night?" Carter surmised, looking at his little cousin Andre.

Grant laughed and looked up at Carter who was an inch or so taller than him. "You could say that."

"I do, because you sure surprised the heck out of all of us with your announcement," Carter replied. "I mean, when you'd asked about Shari in New York, I had no idea that…well, things were that serious between you."

"It didn't take long for those old feelings to resurface," Grant responded. He wasn't eager to discuss his and Shari's relationship, not even with Carter, whom he greatly respected. "If you'll excuse me…" He went out on the dance floor to Shari who'd suddenly become free when her mother had come to take Andre.

"May I have this dance?" Grant asked, holding out his hand to his wife.

Shari's gaze locked in on him. "Of course."

Grant clasped one hand around Shari's small one while the other arm circled her trim waist and landed just above her backside. Slowly, he moved them across the floor in unison.

Shari was a nervous wreck on the dance floor and her heart was like a horse galloping at full speed. She was a bit giddy after drinking so much champagne and only nibbling on her food. She hadn't had an appetite before the wedding or after playing the dewy-eyed adoring bride for the past few hours. Grant hadn't seemed to mind that she rarely left his side. If she hadn't been mistaken, he'd actually seemed to enjoy her company.

And now she was dancing with her handsome husband. He'd never looked better than he did now in his black, two-button tuxedo with tapestry tuxedo vest. His hair was trimmed low and those sexy dimples were irresistible.

Grant was holding her so closely that she could feel his heartbeat. It was beating as fast as hers. What did he have to be excited about? He'd gotten his way. She was his wife now and all that would entail. Speaking of, she had no idea what to expect tonight after the reception. Would Grant want to consummate their marriage? Would she be a convenient body for him to relieve his sexual frustration? Because at this moment, she knew he cared nothing for her. He cared only about Andre.

"You seem to be enjoying yourself," Grant commented after several long excruciatingly painful moments.

"Aren't I supposed to?" she queried, glancing up at him. "I mean, it is our wedding. We're supposed to be happy."

"Yes, we are," Grant said, looking down at her before taking her lips. He used mastery, precision and his tongue to create a soul-shattering kiss that left Shari drained of all thought.

When he raised his head, Shari heard clapping. She blinked several times and noticed her family was watching them. They were lovebirds after all, so Grant planting a kiss on her in the middle of the dance floor was not shocking.

"I think it's time we go," Grant said, whispering in her ear.

"Go?" Shari was perplexed.

"Newlyweds should have a honeymoon."

"Did you forget that *You Take the Cake* is coming to town for a couple of days to follow us around and collect background footage for the show?"

"Ah, yes," Grant said as he rubbed his jaw introspectively, "I had forgotten that. No matter. We'll spend the night at the Drake as I'd planned and I will just postpone our weeklong honeymoon in Hawaii."

"Hawaii?" Shari asked. She hadn't known where he'd planned on taking her for their honeymoon because she'd left all the planning up to him.

"Yes, Hawaii," Grant said, smiling. "If you recall, we're supposed to be madly in love and couldn't wait for a big ceremony and now after such a public display of affection, your family will be thinking we can't wait to be alone in someplace romantic."

Shari was sure Grant felt the exact opposite, but he played up the giddy new husband routine and soon they were heading to a bridal suite to change clothes.

Belinda joined her in one of the rooms. "Wow, that was some ceremony," she said as she helped Shari out of her wedding dress. "I can't believe how well it came together at the last minute."

"It was pretty nice," Shari said as Belinda loosened the bustier straps on the back of her gown so Shari could step out of it.

"So..." Belinda paused. "Are you sure you're ready for this?"

"What do you mean?"

"Well, you haven't been with many men and now you've up and married a man you hardly know." When Shari started to say something, Belinda held her hands up. "I know you had Andre together, but marriage? I just hope you know what you've gotten yourself into."

Shari wasn't sure she did, but what was done was done. She'd made her bed and now she had to lie in it.

Grant knocked on the door several minutes later.

"Come in."

"You ready?" he asked, poking his head into the room.

"She is," Belinda answered for her.

Before she knew it, they were rushing out of the hotel and into a town car that had been decorated with wedding bells and Just Married signs as her family threw birdseed at them. They stopped for a moment to kiss Andre goodbye since he would be staying with her parents for the night.

"See you soon, sweetheart." Shari kissed Andre's cheek before sliding into the backseat. Grant joined her soon after and they were on their way.

## Chapter 7

"Boy, am I glad that's over." Grant unbuttoned the top buttons of his shirt. He'd changed out of his wedding tuxedo into a casual linen suit with a collared shirt. He looked handsome as always and Shari's heart soared.

Shari sat nervously in the seat beside him in the car. They'd chained themselves to each other in an unholy alliance and she wasn't sure what would happen next. Grant didn't seem to care because he leaned his head back and closed his eyes, which signaled to Shari that he wasn't worried about it.

When they arrived at the Drake, the valet opened the car door. "Congratulations," he said to the both of them.

"Thank you." Shari plastered a smile on her face. She hung back and admired the lobby while Grant checked them in.

The Drake Hotel, a Chicago landmark, was just off

the Magnificent Mile. Her mother and aunt had taken her and Belinda there for high tea, and Shari had always been impressed by the classic decor of the hotel. As she looked around the lobby, she was greeted with ornate crown molding, rich brocade fabrics, crystal chandeliers and fresh flower arrangements.

Once Grant obtained their key card, they rode the elevator in silence up to the Princess Diana Suite, and Grant opened the door. He surprised her, though, when he swept her off her feet, into his arms and into the room. Once they cleared the threshold, instead of kissing and making out like most newlyweds, he lowered her back to her feet.

Shari just stared at Grant for several seconds, but he was already moving away. As she walked inside the suite, Shari was impressed with the sumptuous furnishings and luxurious draperies.

"You like?" Grant asked.

"It's lovely," Shari responded, spinning around on her heel. "Looks like you spared no expense."

"Nothing but the best for Mrs. Robinson," Grant said, removing his jacket. He went over to the bar that had been stocked for the evening, poured himself a brandy and took a generous sip.

"Grant, are you regretting your decision to marry me?" Shari asked quietly, taking a seat on a nearby chaise. She couldn't help but notice a hint of derision in his voice.

"No, why would you say that?" he asked, pacing the floor.

Shari shrugged. "You seem a little on edge."

"Yeah, well, today was a long day," Grant replied,

taking another sip of brandy. "You know, keeping up the pretense of being long-lost sweethearts."

"My family seemed to buy it," Shari said. "But I was surprised you didn't invite your family."

"Wasn't time," Grant murmured under his breath.

"Or did you not want them to be there?" Shari asked. "Were you embarrassed of me, of Andre?"

Grant looked as if she'd stabbed a dagger in his heart. He quickly rushed to her side. "Do you really think that?"

"I don't know what to think." Shari shrugged. "I mean they had two weeks. They could have made it. Maybe they didn't want to meet their bastard grandson."

Grant put down his glass and grabbed Shari by the shoulders. "Don't ever say that again. And I'm sorry I said it before. We're a family now and he's got two parents, a mother and a father."

When Shari winced at Grant's strong arms, he relinquished his harsh grasp. "Sorry. Listen, that's not why I didn't invite them."

"Then why?" Shari pressed.

"My parents and I don't have a good relationship like you and your parents. They would have brought us nothing but anxiety. My father would have tried to be the boss and my mother would have wanted everything her way. Once we get back from L.A., we'll invite them for a visit and they can spend some time with their grandson."

Shari nodded and stifled a yawn.

"See," he pointed out to her, "I told you it was a long day. Why don't we go to bed?"

Shari's heart lurched. *Go to bed?* Did he mean to—

gether? Grant didn't say, instead, he rose to his feet and then asked, "Would you like to go first?"

"Oh, yes," she said, rising from the sofa. She grabbed her overnight bag and rushed into the master bath. It was elegantly decorated and fit for royalty—no, make that fit for two. The clawfoot tub sat regally in the center of the room, big enough for a couple of lovebirds, while the walk-in shower could easily fit several people.

Shari took her time in the bathroom, brushing her teeth and changing out of the simple white sheath she'd been wearing into a white chiffon negligee with ruffles that stopped at her thigh. She'd received it as a gift from Belinda for her wedding night when she, Lorraine and Monica had taken her out for a bridal shower. Shari wasn't sure whether she would need it or not, so she slid the matching chiffon robe around her and tied it around her middle. When she was sure she'd wasted enough time and Grant had fallen asleep, she emerged, only to find him wide awake and sitting up in an accent chair. "All done." She gave a hesitant smile.

Grant openly stared at her from beneath hooded lashes for several long, aching minutes before jumping off the couch. With the lustful look he'd given her, Shari had thought he was coming to take her to bed, but all she heard was a growl and some words muttered under his breath before he'd stalked into the master bath and slammed the door.

While Grant busied himself in the bathroom, Shari snuck into the master bedroom and slid underneath the covers. Although they'd had an interlude in her house after the Cubs game, she wasn't altogether sure she was ready to consummate their relationship. She hadn't been with many men since Grant—only two others to be exact. Andre took too much of her time, so she wasn't very skilled in the bedroom department.

Grant was a gorgeous, sexy bachelor, who'd probably been with dozens of women. Shari was sure he was used to women who knew how to please a man in the bedroom. With her limited experience, Shari felt woefully inept.

When Grant finally exited, he was bare chested and wearing silk pajama bottoms. He was buffer than he'd been in college and looked even more powerful now. His chest looked like it had been chiseled out of stone. Shari's heart began pounding in her chest at the mere sight of her half-naked husband. She didn't know how she was going to sleep with that image of Grant in her head.

Before she could utter a single word, Grant said, "I will be sleeping on the sofa in the living room." He grabbed two pillows off the bed, stuffed them under his arms and left the room.

Any hopes or secret desires Shari had about having a real marriage with Grant was dashed when he walked out of the bedroom on their wedding night, leaving her horny as hell. She was going to have a tense, lonely night in her honeymoon bed looking up at the ceiling and waiting for morning to come.

Grant plunged hard and deep inside her hot, moist sheath. Shari arched her hips up to meet him and clenched to take more and more of him in. She gripped the back of his head as he pulled out only to thrust in again. Her breathing became more rapid as Grant whispered, "Come with me, baby," and their bodies began to rock in steady cadence. An intense orgasm shook Shari to the very core and she woke up with a start only to find Grant staring down at her holding a cup of coffee.

"Must have been some dream," Grant replied, smiling devilishly. "You were moaning in your sleep."

Shari colored. She wanted to crawl up in the covers and die. The dream had seemed so real, so vivid. She'd thought she'd been making love to Grant. Was it a wish-fulfillment dream? she wondered. And how noisy had she been? "I...I, uh..." She had no words.

Grant smiled mischievously and offered her the other cup in his hand. "This might help you wake up."

"Thank you." Shari accepted the proffered mug and lowered her head. She drank liberally, eager to wake herself out of her sex-induced daze. She couldn't speak. What could she say? He probably realized that she'd been dreaming about having sex. Now, whether he knew that he was the intended recipient was another matter entirely.

"About last night," Grant began.

Shari shook her head as she sat up. She used one hand to push the pillows back while holding the coffee cup. She didn't really want to have this conversation. "You really don't have to explain. You want a marriage of convenience. I understand the ground rules."

"There are no ground rules," Grant said, sipping his coffee. "We're in this marriage for the long haul. And I want fidelity. I don't want you sleeping with someone else. So at some point, one or both of us might want more and...and let's just let nature take its course, okay? No expectations."

What Grant was saying sounded fair and logical, but when it came to matters of the heart or lust, logic rarely ruled. Still, Shari asked, "Do you think a real marriage between us is possible?"

"I don't know," Grant said, "but I certainly hope so. Otherwise, forever is going to be a long time."

That was an understatement, Grant thought after he'd dropped Shari back home so she could change and go into Lillian's while he was preparing to pack up some things to take to her house.

His penthouse—with breakable pieces of art, vases and sharp edges—was no place for a growing boy. He was going to have to change his life entirely because he was about to be a full-time father. Gone were the days of gallivanting at the drop of a hat. There was someone, namely his wife and son, waiting for him. He also had the daunting task of relocating the Robinson Restaurants headquarters from New York to Chicago.

He still couldn't believe that he and Shari were married. Their sudden marriage still felt like a dream to him…until she walked out of their honeymoon suite at the Drake wearing that barely there, see-through chemise. Didn't she know that she was playing with fire? It had taken everything in him not to rip the slip of fabric off her body and pin her underneath him until she was moaning like she'd been that morning. *Is that how she would sound if I was buried deep inside her?*

He'd been surprised this morning to find her writhing in their marital bed. Had she been dreaming of him? If so, he would have liked nothing better than to make her fantasy a reality.

His body said yes, go for it, but his mind cautioned him about getting involved with Shari too soon, too fast. She'd lost his trust and was going to have to earn it back. So he had to keep her at arm's length, but for how long, he didn't know. Grant surmised he could so long as he could keep his desires for her at bay. Moving into her home wasn't going to make that choice any easier, but he was determined to try. Shari had to know that she couldn't deceive him for half a decade without consequences. The problem was in punishing her, he was also punishing himself.

"I'm surprised to see you back to work so soon," Belinda said when Shari walked into the kitchen at Lillian's that morning. "I would have thought that gorgeous husband of yours would have kept you in bed for days."

"You do remember we have the *You Take the Cake* crew coming to film us today," Shari replied, putting on her apron. "For background for the show."

"Of course I remember," Belinda said as she decorated some cookies with frosting. "I just assumed you weren't coming. I mean, you did just get married yesterday and all."

"I would never miss this," Shari replied huffily. "This competition is as important to me as it is to the rest of you."

"The rest of us what?" Carter asked, walking into the kitchen, several minutes late as always. He stared at his two cousins and then turned to Shari. "And what are you doing here, anyway? Shouldn't you be on your honeymoon?"

Belinda gave Shari an *I told you so* look.

"In case you guys forgot, Grandma asked all of us to be present for this background piece," Shari reminded them.

"Are you sure there's nothing more to the story?" Belinda asked.

Shari sighed. "There's nothing more other than wanting to be a part of the show like everyone else. Speaking of Grandma, is she around?" Shari changed the subject. She in no way wanted to get in a conversation about her marriage with her family. Otherwise, they might start to see the obvious holes.

"No, not yet."

"I have to say, you looked beautiful yesterday, kid," Carter told Shari, kissing her on the forehead. "You've never looked lovelier."

Shari smiled broadly. "Thank you."

After the initial fuss over Shari's sudden emergence after one night of honeymooning, they all got to work. Soon, they were baking cakes, cookies, cupcakes and pastries for the day.

When they'd started making a custom cake for a six-year-old with a carousel theme, they were interrupted by her aunt Daisy and Shari's father. "They're here, they're here," her aunt said, rushing into the kitchen.

Shari wiped the sweat off her forehead with her towel. "Oh, my goodness, how do I look?" she asked. She turned and looked at Belinda, who was asking her the exact same question.

"I don't know why the two of you are getting all bent out of shape," Belinda's fiancé, Malik, said from her side. "I think they want to see us in our natural habitat, you know, working, not perfectly made-up."

"That doesn't mean we want flour on our faces," Shari responded. She had only had a few minutes to check her hair and lipstick in the restroom before the

*You Take the Cake* crew came into the kitchen, bringing with them lots of noise and commotion.

There was Brandon Tyler, whom Shari recognized immediately as the host of *You Take the Cake*. He was a young, slender man with pompadour hair, who couldn't be more than twenty-five. He was wearing jeans, a plaid shirt with a blazer over it. Then there was a director and several cameramen; one held a camera on his shoulder, another was holding a boom.

"Everyone, this is Drew Campbell," her father said. "He is the supervising director of *You Take the Cake* and will be helping facilitate the interviews today with Brandon here." Her father smiled at the host.

"Thank you, Mr. Drayson," Drew said. "We're here today to meet Miss Lillian, get some background on the bakery and to interview all of you who help make this place a success."

Over the next couple of hours, Brandon interviewed each of them individually, Belinda and Drake, Carter and Shari and even Malik since they were the primary bakers. They were finishing up when Grandma Lillian and Monica came in.

"Perfect timing," Brandon replied when he saw Lillian Drayson. "The matriarch of the family has arrived." He walked toward her and when he reached her, he kissed her hand. "A pleasure, Mrs. Drayson. I hear you've been running this bakery for over fifty years. And from what several of the customers have said, it's a Chicago institution."

Grandma Lillian smiled. "Yes, it is. I've prided myself in producing the best in gourmet baking the city of Chicago has to offer."

"Well, your grandchildren have certainly inherited

your gift," Brandon replied. "We've already been able to film several of their works of art." He motioned to the cake creations on the counter. "Not to mention sampled some of them."

Grandma Lillian smiled at her brood, and Shari couldn't help but feel proud. They had done a fine job upholding the family tradition. She knew her grandmother was sure that this competition was the right thing to bring them all closer together. She was ready to retire and allow one or more of her grandchildren to take over the business. Shari only hoped it would be her.

When Shari arrived home, she was surprised to see Grant and Andre on the floor playing Connect Four. How the hell had he gotten in?

"Look who's home," Grant said to Andre by his side.

Andre quickly jumped up from the floor and plowed into her arms. "Mommy, Mommy. Daddy came to get me from Grandma's house and we went to the movies."

*Daddy.* Had Andre really gotten this attached, this fast? Had Andre wanted a dad all this time and she'd just been oblivious to his needs?

"That's wonderful, sweetheart." Shari planted a kiss on his forehead. "I was just about to shower and go pick you up, but I see I needn't have worried about that."

Grant looked bashful. "I'm sorry. I should have called, but when I tried you earlier to ask, you were busy with the television crew and I didn't want to interrupt. How did it go?"

"It went good," Shari said. "They interviewed all of us and Grandma Lillian. There's even talk about following a few of us around once we arrive in L.A."

"Sounds exciting," Grant said, lifting himself off the floor.

"It was," Shari said as she retreated to her bedroom and began to undress. She didn't know what to make of the situation. Grant had just made himself comfortable in her home as if he belonged there. With the swiftness in which they'd gotten married, they really hadn't had a chance to discuss their living arrangements, and now Shari wasn't sure how to react. Having Grant in her personal space was disconcerting; his larger-than-life presence seemed to fill up the entire house.

"We'll finish playing later on, little man. Your mama and I are going to have a little chat," she heard Grant say. When she turned around, she was surprised to find Grant standing directly behind her, in her bedroom. At six feet, he loomed in her doorway, looking incredibly sexy in a polo shirt and jeans. Grant had a vitality that was inherently masculine.

"Grant!" She placed her hands to cover her chest, but she could do little else standing in her Skivvies.

"Sorry, I didn't mean to startle you," Grant said, but he didn't stop staring at her, either.

"Was that before or after you moved yourself into my house?"

Grant's mouth curled into a frown. "Did you expect for us to live apart?" he inquired. "I told you I wasn't going to spend another minute away from my son than absolutely necessary."

"Yeah, well you could have at least asked me," Shari replied, turning her back to him and reaching for her robe, which was lying across the foot of her bed. "You just moved yourself in here without a word or any discussion. And how did you even get in here, anyway, let alone pick up Andre?"

"I am his father. I have every right to pick him up."

Shari shook her head. This conversation was quickly deteriorating. He was right, of course, but she'd been Andre's mother and his sole guardian for the past four years. She hadn't been prepared for Grant to jump in so fast. "You're right. And I know that, but can you give me a minute to adjust? All of this—" she pointed to the two of them "—is happening so quickly. I…I can't seem to catch my breath."

Grant walked into her bedroom, making the room feel that much smaller. "Do you think you're the only one, Shari? In the span of two weeks, I've gained a wife and a son. I have to move my home base for Robinson Restaurants to Chicago, put my penthouse up for sale. Hell, my whole life is changing and I'm trying to roll with the punches. And you're going to have to do the same, Shari. Our living together is nonnegotiable. I want to get to know my son and for him to get to know me. Surely you can appreciate that."

Shari sighed. "Of course I do. And I can see that Andre has taken to you. I'm not blind, okay? It's just going to take some time for me to adjust to living with someone."

"There's no time better than the present," Grant said, pulling the polo shirt he was wearing over his head to reveal a wifebeater underneath.

Shari's mouth hung open when he began unzipping his jeans. "What—what are you doing?"

"I'm changing into something more comfortable." He opened up her closet and pulled out some sweats.

When had he put clothes in her closet?

"Dinner is on the way," Grant continued, stepping out of his jeans. "I ordered some Chinese and it should be here any minute. I figured after a long day that you might not be in the mood to cook."

Shari was shocked by not only Grant's state of undress and seeing him in his boxer briefs, but by his thoughtfulness. "Thank you," she said, turning her head away. "But can't you change in the bathroom?"

"I could, but since I'll be sleeping in here tonight, you might as well get used to my presence." He slipped the sweatpants over his muscled thighs.

"You're sleeping here?" Shari managed to croak out.

Grant eyed her. "Where else? This is a small house and I don't want Andre asking questions. Married couples sleep together so that's what we're going to do."

Given her burning attraction to him, Shari didn't know how she was going to sleep next to him night after night with no release. "Fine." She was tired of fighting. "But I'll change in the bathroom." Seconds later, when she was in the safety of her master bath, she leaned against the door and prayed for inner strength.

When she emerged after a quick shower and change of clothes, Shari found Grant and Andre sitting at the kitchen table surrounded by cartons of Chinese food.

"Is there any food left for me?" she asked with a rueful smile.

"Absolutely." Grant pulled out the chair next to him and Shari sat down beside him.

And together, they laughed, talked and shared their first dinner as a family.

## Chapter 8

Two days later they were on their way to Los Angeles. Shari hadn't expected Grant to accompany her on the trip since he was relocating his corporate office, but he'd been insistent that he didn't want to be separated from his family. Shari suspected he meant Andre, so she'd accepted the inevitable rather than fight with Grant.

And so the entire family, including her husband and son boarded an early morning flight and arrived in the afternoon. The sun was shining brightly without a cloud in the sky when the Drayson family arrived. *You Take the Cake* had sent several limousines to take the family to a swanky hotel in Beverly Hills where they'd be staying along with the other bakeries—Bliss, Sweet Tastings, Delovely Cakemakers, Double Yum Bakers and of course Brown Sugar Bakery. There were now two additional bakeries competing, thanks to an outpouring of calls and emails from fans who wanted to include these two well-known bakeries. So the show had decided to expand the competition from a one-day event to a weeklong competition to raise the stakes.

Shari wasn't looking forward to having to face Dina again after all these years, but at least this time she hadn't come up short. She was wearing Grant's ring on her finger and this time, Dina would be envious of Shari.

She was so deep in her own thoughts that she didn't hear Andre's comment until he shook her and said, "L.A. has so many palm trees."

"Yes, they do," Shari said from his side. She'd allowed Andre to have the window seat in the limousine and was sandwiched in between him and Grant. She was so close to Grant that she could smell his aftershave.

When they arrived at the hotel, she and Grant received a suite, as did several other members of the family. Everyone went their separate ways, promising to reconvene for dinner later that night when the television crew would come to film them for a clip that showed their family solidarity. Grandma Lillian had given them all a prep talk at the family estate that they had all better get along. Everyone had agreed to be on their best behavior or incur Grandma's wrath.

At dinner, Grant was the consummate actor. He played the role of devoted newlywed for the cameras, so much so that Shari wondered if her cousins would get upset that the show was paying too much attention to them and not the rest of the family. But everyone was getting along good-naturedly.

Shari found it easy to respond to Grant's charms,

especially when his hand rested on the small of her back or when he looked at her like she was the only woman in the room. No, no, no, it was when he kissed her. His kisses were becoming a regular occurrence and when he brushed his mouth softly across hers, her lips would part of their own volition and open to him, causing fireworks to explode inside her body. After a few of their kisses, he looked at her oddly; he must have felt the sensations, too. It made her secretly wonder if there could be more between them than just this illusion they'd created for the world to see. Grant had indicated he was open to exploring a real marriage with her. Truth be told, it was what Shari was hoping for, praying for. They'd been denied their chance to be a family because of Dina's machinations. Their marriage had to work!

The next couple of days, Shari, Grant and Andre played tourist. They visited a children's museum before hopping on a tour bus to visit the Grauman's Chinese Theatre, Dolby Theatre and to walk down the boulevard looking at the stars' names.

On their last day before filming they went to Santa Monica Beach. Andre had never seen an ocean. Living in Chicago, he'd only seen Lake Michigan, so Shari had donned a simple two-piece bathing suit and Grant his trunks, and they'd rented an umbrella and loungers so they could help Andre make sand castles on the beach.

She noticed Grant eyeing her in her print tankini. Shari wasn't comfortable in a bikini like most of the women in Los Angeles, but Grant seemed to appreciate her figure. His eyes roved the swell of her breasts just visible in the tank top and the curve of her backside when she turned over to fish for her book in her purse.

Shari acted like she hadn't noticed and pulled her deliciously sexy romance novel over her face, but every so often she would catch Grant's eyes on her. Eventually, he and Andre ended up splashing around in the ocean. She looked up when she heard the sound of their laughter. She'd never seen Andre so happy, so content. And Grant…well, he looked like he was enjoying being a big kid. After the beach, they ended their day with a walk on the Santa Monica Pier. They stopped long enough for Andre to play at Pacific Park. They rode bumper cars, played carnival games and Grant played Skeeball and won Andre a huge stuffed lion, his favorite animal.

When they finally strode back into the hotel after two days of playing tourist, Shari was exhausted. After taking a quick shower, she crawled into bed with Grant. She'd finally put Andre down after he'd talked her ear off about how much fun he'd had.

"That son of ours has lots of energy," Grant said, holding the covers so Shari could slide in beside him.

"Yes, he does," Shari agreed, punching her pillow to fluff it. She'd gotten used to sleeping next to Grant the past few days, having his strong, muscled body next to her. Despite their lack of intimacy, his presence was oddly comforting.

"I don't know who's more tired—me or him."

"Both," Shari offered.

"Are you ready for tomorrow?" Grant inquired, turning on his side to face her.

Shari looked up at the ceiling. She knew what he was asking, even though he hadn't said it. Was she ready to see Dina again after all these years?

"As ready as I can be," she finally said, glancing in his direction. Brown Sugar Bakery was Lillian's fiercest competition, and Shari and the entire Drayson family had no intention of having Dina stand in their way for the win.

After sleeping in the next morning, Shari found the entire clan downstairs in the lobby. Grandma Lillian, Grandpa Henry, her parents and sister Monica, Aunt Daisy and Uncle Matt and her cousins Drake, Belinda and Carter, and Malik. They were all wearing their pink and brown Lillian's T-shirts. Her stomach churned in nervous anticipation, so Shari decided to forego breakfast.

"You ready?" Belinda asked when she saw Shari.

"Yes, why do you ask?"

"You look a little tense."

"I'm fine. I'm fine," Shari replied.

"Everyone ready to go?" Drake asked. "The limousines are here."

Thirty minutes later, they were at the *You Take the Cake* studio. The director led them into the kitchen where they would be filming. The other competitors—Bliss, Sweet Tastings, Delovely Cakemakers, Double Yum Bakers and Brown Sugar Bakery were already there. Each of them had several members to their team, but none of them were as large as the Drayson clan. Shari was proud as she stood in unison with her family. They were a force to be reckoned with.

Who she didn't see was Dina. Typical! Dina was going to make an entrance. Why did she always have to be the center of attention?

"If you excuse me for a minute," Shari said to Carter, who was standing at her side. "I'm going to the restroom." She walked the long corridor, pushed open the wooden doors and came face-to-face with Dina English.

"Shari." Dina's eyes grew large when Shari walked into the restroom and she stopped powdering her nose.

Dina had matured into a classic beauty, with fair skin and hair down to her shoulders. She wore skinny jeans, a crisp, white baking smock that read *Brown Sugar Bakery* and platform shoes. No cheap T-shirt for her. With her flawless makeup, Dina was as gorgeous as ever.

"Dina." Shari knew this day was coming—the day she'd have to face her nemesis after five years. But what surprised her most was that the anger and hurt she'd felt all those years ago at losing Grant to Dina came rushing back hard and fast at just laying eyes on her former best friend.

"You look really good," Dina replied, attempting to make light conversation.

Shari didn't answer. She merely went into the stall. She was hoping Dina would just go away, but no such luck. When she reemerged, Dina was still there, waiting for her.

"I was hoping we could talk," Dina said. "You know, before the competition starts." She placed her compact back in her purse and snapped it shut. She turned around to face Shari.

"I have nothing to say to you, Dina." Shari washed her hands, careful not to make eye contact with the woman.

"Now, I know you're lying," Dina responded. "I've known you a long time, Shari Drayson, and I can tell when you're lying."

Shari spun on her heels and spat out, "You don't know the first thing about me, Dina."

Dina held up her hands in a defensive mode. "Whoa! I knew you were upset with me, but…"

"But what?" Shari said, walking closer toward Dina until their faces were inches apart. "You didn't think I'd be upset that you stole from my family or that you stole Grant from me?"

"I didn't steal Grant," Dina responded, stepping backward. "He was never yours to begin with. You weren't in a relationship."

"That's right," Shari said, pointing to Dina. "And you saw to that, didn't you? As soon as you saw that we'd slept together, you sunk your claws into him as fast as you could."

"Grant was a great catch," Dina replied. "And although you had a crush on him, you never made a play for him."

"I slept with him!" Fury boiled within Shari at Dina's gall.

"Yes, but then you told him it was a hookup, that it meant nothing. *You* left the door wide open for me and I walked through it. You have no one to blame but yourself. *You* let him go. If he'd been in my bed, there would have been no way I'd have let him go. You didn't know what to do with a man like Grant. He needed a real woman, someone confident, and I stepped up to the plate."

Dina's words stung. She was tapping into all Shari's insecurities about how she wasn't good enough. "You knew I had feelings for Grant, but you wanted him for yourself and you weren't going to let our nearly four-year friendship stand in your way. Whatever it took, right?"

"Shari, listen…" Dina began, but Shari interrupted her and held her hand up.

"Well, your machinations to keep us apart didn't work, Dina."

"What are you talking about?"

"I know you told Grant that Thomas was going to propose to me and wanted a virgin bride. You told Grant that if he pursued me he would ruin my life, my future. What other lies did you tell Grant to convince him to date you?"

"That's ridiculous." Dina laughed derisively, not admitting what she'd done. "Why are we rehashing the past, anyway? What's done is done. I married Grant." She turned to walk away, but Shari grabbed her arm.

"We are not finished yet," Shari said. "Because I have not had my say. You did nearly ruin my life, Dina. Thanks to you I had to have my son—*Grant's* son— alone."

Shari watched as horror spread across Dina's face. She looked as if she'd been punched in the gut. "Son?"

Shari nodded. "Yes. My one-night stand with Grant produced a child, who, thanks to you, grew up without a father."

"I…I had no idea you were pregnant," Dina responded. "No idea at all. I would never have…you know how hard it was for me not having my father around after my parents divorced."

"Don't you worry about my son because your plan to keep Grant and me apart didn't work. We're a family now." Shari held up her left hand to show Dina her platinum wedding band and then headed toward the door.

"Wait!" Dina said, but Shari cut her off.

We'd like to send you two free books to introduce you to Kimani™ Romance books. These novels feature strong, sexy women, and African-American heroes that are charming, loving and true. Our authors fill each page with exceptional dialogue, exciting plot twists, and enough sizzling romance to keep you riveted until the very end!

*KIMANI ROMANCE...LOVE'S ULTIMATE DESTINATION*

Your two books have combined cover pric of $13 in the U.S. or $14.50 in Canada, bu are yours **FREE!**

We'll even send you two wonderful surprise gifts. You can't lose!

# THE EDITOR'S "THANK YOU" FREE GIFTS INCLUDE:

➤ Two Kimani™ Romance Novels
➤ Two exciting surprise gifts

YES! I have placed my Editor's "thank you" Free Gifts seal in the space provided at right. Please send me 2 FREE Books, and my 2 FREE Mystery Gifts. I understand that I am under no obligation to purchase anything further, as explained on the back of this card.

PLACE FREE GIFTS SEAL HERE

## 168/368 XDL FV32

*Please Print*

FIRST NAME

LAST NAME

ADDRESS

APT.#                    CITY

STATE/PROV.              ZIP/POSTAL CODE

## Thank You!

# ♦ HARLEQUIN® READER SERVICE—Here's How It Works:

Accepting your 2 free books and 2 free gifts (gifts valued at approximately $10.00) places you under no obligation to buy anything. You may keep the books and gifts and return the shipping statement marked "cancel." If you do not cancel, about a month later we'll send you 4 additional books and bill you just $5.19 each in the U.S. or $5.49 each in Canada. That is a savings of at least 20% off the cover price. Shipping and handling is just 50¢ per book in the U.S. and 75¢ per book in Canada.* You may cancel at any time, but if you choose to continue, every month we'll send you 4 more books, which you may either purchase at the discount price or return to us and cancel your subscription.
*Terms and prices subject to change without notice. Prices do not include applicable taxes. Sales tax applicable in N.Y. Canadian residents will be charged applicable taxes. Offer not valid in Quebec. All orders subject to credit approval. Credit or debit balances in a customer's account(s) may be offset by any other outstanding balance owed by or to the customer. Offer available while quantities last. Books received may not be as shown. Please allow 4 to 6 weeks for delivery.

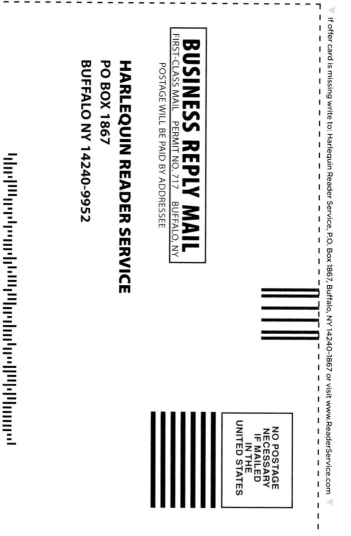

If offer card is missing write to: Harlequin Reader Service, P.O. Box 1867, Buffalo, NY 14240-1867 or visit www.ReaderService.com

BUSINESS REPLY MAIL
FIRST-CLASS MAIL    PERMIT NO. 717    BUFFALO, NY

POSTAGE WILL BE PAID BY ADDRESSEE

HARLEQUIN READER SERVICE
PO BOX 1867
BUFFALO NY 14240-9952

NO POSTAGE
NECESSARY
IF MAILED
IN THE
UNITED STATES

"I have nothing further to say to you. Other than may the best bakery win. And make no doubt about it, it will be Lillian's."

Shari willed herself to calm down as she walked back into the kitchen, but her blood was boiling. She knew her face had to beet-red because Dina had pushed all her buttons. Dina had pretty much implied that it was her fault that Andre didn't have a father. Was she right? Even if she had wanted to get involved with Grant after that night together, Dina had jumped on him so fast, Shari hadn't had a chance to tell him her true feelings. Perhaps if she'd been confident back then, she wouldn't have allowed Dina to get in her way.

"There you are." Grandma Lillian came rushing toward her. "Where have you been? The director was going over all the details of the challenge."

"I'm here now, Grandma."

"I need you focused, Shari," she urged, tugging Shari's arm along. "That's the key to winning this thing. I can't have your mind elsewhere."

"You don't have to worry," Shari responded, patting her grandmother's arm as Dina entered the room. She saw Dina looking her way. She was clearly as shaken up as Shari by their encounter in the ladies' restroom, but Shari had to ignore her. "I will give it everything I've got. We will win this competition."

"You all have been chosen as the best bakers in America," Brandon Tyler, the host, said. "And we're going to put you to the test."

"We're up for it!" Carter said enthusiastically. Several of the other bakery teams concurred.

"That's good." Brandon smiled. "Because we will be testing your ability to work under pressure but still deliver a quality product. It's all about creativity, taste and of course your presentation."

"Brown Sugar Bakery is all about creativity," Dina boasted from the sidelines. "We got this." She bumped shoulders with several members of her team while the Drayson family gave her the evil eye.

Brandon continued, "Since you're the best of the best, we've really amped up our challenge."

"What does the show have in mind?" Grandma Lillian asked.

"It is 'Cakes Around the World' week," Brandon announced excitedly. "Instead of one day, it'll be a weeklong challenge. Every day you'll be asked to create a cake from around the world with a few curveballs here and there."

"Wow!" Drake said from beside Shari. "We certainly hadn't thought about that."

"Don't worry, Drake," his sister Belinda replied. "With all the talent we have, we can handle anything they throw our way."

"So if you guys are ready…" Brandon said. "Let the competition begin!"

Each team was given a few minutes to figure out who would be working for the day. The Drayson family formed a football huddle to determine who would go up against their competitors. Deciding they'd get a really hard country to start off the show, they'd settled on Carter, Malik and Shari for the first day.

Shari heard everything that was said, but every time she got excited, she would turn to find Dina staring at her curiously.

"Is everything okay here?" Carter asked, coming to her side.

"Why would you ask?"

"Because if looks could kill, judging by the looks that have been passing between you and Dina, we'd all be dead," Carter replied.

Shari scoffed, "It's been five years since we last saw each other. What did you expect? For us to skip and hold hands like a bunch of schoolgirls? Too much has happened, Carter. Too much that can't be forgotten."

"Is this all about Grant?" he pressed.

"I don't want to talk about it," Shari said. She doubted she would ever fully be able to get over Dina's betrayal.

Carter held up his hands in protest. "Okay. Okay. I'll leave it be."

The director, Drew, walked them through their markers and what would be expected of them. He advised them that the ovens had all been preheated and the pantries and refrigerators stocked with whatever they might need for the day. He cautioned them that it would be a long shoot each day.

"Today, we want you to transport us to the romantic country of France," the host said.

Carter gave the rest of the family standing on the sidelines the thumbs-up signal. With his skills and Shari's delicate pastry skills they were a cinch in this round. "Your first challenge is to incorporate the mystery ingredient sitting in the box at each of your countertops into your miniature cakes," Brandon added. "And remember, we'll be looking for creativity, taste and presentation. We'll give you a few minutes to deliberate."

"It's as we thought," Carter replied. "So I was thinking we could do a *dacquoise.*"

"And a *mille-feuille,*" Shari replied. She knew her Napoleon with layers of puff pastry and pastry cream would be a winner.

"Sounds good to me," Malik added.

The first and subsequent rounds that day were long. They impressed the judges with the creamy texture of Carter's *dacquoise* filled with hazelnut meringue and chocolate buttercream. Dina's Brown Sugar Bakery did several different petit fours, Bliss made a chocolate Charlotte with brandy-soaked ladyfingers, Delovely did a lemon soufflé and Double Yum did an apple *tarte Tatin,* which the judges loved. The bakery eliminated was Sweet Tastings. The bakery had done a version of a Napoleon, but theirs was not nearly as good as Shari's.

"You guys did fantastic!" Grandma Lillian said at the end of the day as they were cleaning up their stations.

"Was that as easy as it looked?" Shari's father asked her.

"Not in the slightest," Shari said, wiping the sweat off her brow with the back of her hand. The day had been physically as well as emotionally draining. They'd been taping for nearly ten hours.

A couple of times she'd seen Dina eyeing what they were doing. Shari was trying her best to ignore the woman, but she could see that Dina was impressed with just how far Lillian's had come since she'd left them. The Drayson family had become more skilled and adept at their craft, and they'd added several new products to their repertoire.

"You guys were definitely on point," Drake said once

the day was over. "We'll have to add a couple of those recipes to the *Brothers Who Bake* cookbook."

"So long as this sista," Shari added, "gets a shout-out. These two—" she punched Carter and Malik in the arm "—were not the only ones in that kitchen."

"Of course, cuz," Drake said, pulling Shari into a hug and ruffling her hair. He was so much taller than she was that he towered over her at six feet tall. "We couldn't do it without you."

Grant was glad to have the day to himself. Ever since they'd come to Los Angeles, he'd had to play the role of a newlywed who adored his wife. The role was becoming easier and easier because if he admitted it to himself, he was enjoying Shari's company and kissing her and feeling her soft lips against his.

The days spent with her and Andre had been wonderful. He was beginning to learn what his son liked and disliked, but the nights…oh, the endless nights of lying beside Shari in bed were driving him crazy. He wanted to make love to her until she was moaning in ecstasy. He didn't know how he was going to be able to continue to restrain himself from taking her in his arms.

Instead, he'd focused on business while Andre watched cartoons. He had a conference call with several of his restaurant managers discussing staffing, menus and orders. His flagship restaurant in New York was looking for a temporary executive chef because the current one had unexpectedly taken maternity leave when she'd given birth at eight months. Solange was an excellent chef and would be hard to replace even if on a temporary basis. They had their work cut out for them.

A few hours later, he was taking Andre out for the

day because his son was getting antsy being indoors. He took Andre to the Los Angeles Zoo and Botanical Gardens. The zoo had hands-on activities, stories and live animal encounters for children of Andre's age. They explored the zoo's grounds and animal collection from the fabulous flamingos to lovable chimpanzees to the ginormous giraffes. In amazement, Grant watched Andre's fearlessness. His son, unlike other children, was not intimidated, easily petting the animals when allowed in the children's petting zoo. Andre laughed with joy when he rode the new carousel in the center of the zoo.

Grant was glad he had this time with Andre. It was important to him that he develop a relationship with his son that was separate from Shari. He had a lot of time to make up for. Andre was too young for him to ask him how he felt about having a sudden father, but Grant wanted him to know he was loved and important in his world, just as important as Shari.

Ah, there she went again, creeping into his thoughts. He'd done a good job of keeping his thoughts of her at bay throughout the day. But the day was over and Shari would be back soon, playing the dutiful wife and wearing those sexy jeans or the floral fragrance that filled his nostrils. He was on the edge and all it was going to take was one push to make him act on his desires.

Shari went through the motions as she sat beside Grant and Andre at a late dinner in the hotel with her family. She gave all the appropriate responses when asked a question, but her mind was a million miles away. Despite her lack of interest, the entire Drayson family was poised for tomorrow.

"We have to beat Dina," Carter was saying when Grandma Lillian interrupted him.

"Winning isn't everything," she said. When several family members looked doubtful, she clarified her remark. "Of course I want Lillian's to win, but as long as we do our best, give it our all, that's all that truly matters."

"C'mon, Grandma," Drake responded incredulously. "We can't let Dina win. Not after all the training you gave her. Not when she stole some of our recipes to start her own bakery."

"We don't know that for sure," Grandma replied.

"Did you see her website?" Drake asked. "Her almond macaroon cake looks awfully like Lillian's."

"I'd have to agree with Drake, Grandma," Belinda added. "Look at what she did to Shari."

All eyes at the table suddenly turned to Shari. She looked up from her plate to questioning eyes. "Do we have to rehash this yet again?" Without another word, she rose from the table and headed out of the restaurant.

Shari didn't go up to her room immediately. She couldn't bear the sexual tension and emotional turmoil between her and Grant. She took a short walk along the boulevard before finally returning to their room nearly an hour later.

"Where have you been?" Grant said, jumping off the couch in the en suite and coming toward her. "I was worried sick when I didn't find you in the room."

"I'm sorry to make you worry." Shari's voice broke and then she rushed into the master bedroom. She flung herself onto the bed and the tears she'd been holding in came spilling out.

Grant was beside her within seconds. He was stroking her hair softly and whispering her name. "Did something happen today, my love? Whatever happened, I promise you, it'll get better."

"Dina," she muttered. And then she paused. Did Grant just call her *my love?*

He lowered his head until he was inches away from her face and wiped her tears away with the tips of his fingers. "Shari, my love," he said.

There. He'd said it again and this time, she hadn't imagined it.

She turned around to face him and that was long enough for Grant to slant his mouth possessively over hers. He brushed his lips softly over Shari's and he kissed her as if she was made of glass and might break.

Shari opened her eyes for mere seconds. That's when Grant lifted his head to look down at her. He seemed to be intuitively asking her if she wanted him to stop.

Something unraveled inside her. *Don't let me go.*

She was feeling a little bruised and battered after her encounter with Dina earlier. She wanted, no needed to be held, to be kissed, to be adored.

When she didn't speak, he leaned down to kiss her again. This time, he traced every inch of her mouth with his tongue. He teased the corners and she opened her mouth up to him and when she did, torrid sensations filled her body. Her heart spurred in a fast, frantic beat.

Grant used the opportunity to deepen the kiss, sealing his mouth and hot tongue over hers. He slid his hands leisurely up and down her body as his tongue toyed hungrily with hers and he made love to her mouth. He dragged his mouth from her lips and up her jaw to her ear. Using his teeth, he gently nipped on her earlobe and a moan escaped her lips. The floodgates of emotion that she'd kept at bay the last couple of weeks—heck, the last five years—opened.

Grant rolled to his knees in one fluid movement. He rose from the bed and gazed down at her with wicked desire, and she knew he was hers for tonight. He undressed her tenderly, slowly, reverently.

"Simply beautiful," he said, his eyes raking over every inch of her body. When he'd stripped her naked to her birthday suit, he pulled his shirt out of his pants and began unbuttoning each button ever so slowly.

Shari took a sharp intake of breath when his shirt fell down to the floor, and she was able to lay eyes on his bare chest again. She swallowed hard, but that didn't stop her from allowing her eyes to sweep over him as he'd done her. Her gaze zeroed in on his erection straining in his pants as she watched him unbuckle them. She released a deep sigh when he eased them and his briefs down his muscular thighs in one fell swoop.

He returned to the bed, and she entwined her hands around his neck, opened her mouth and wrapped her legs around him. Every cell in her body wanted to be touched by this man, to become one with him. When she felt his hardness nudging against her thigh, she moved against him, desperate to be closer to him.

Grant broke his mouth away and trailed a hot, wet kiss down her neck to her bosom. Shari thrust her breasts forward, eager for his touch. Grant easily obliged. He cupped her breasts and they pressed in his palms and Shari gasped.

"Yes," she said through heavy-lidded lashes.

He rolled one nipple, plucking the tip between his fingers and Shari arched against his touch. He continued the sensual onslaught by taking the distended bud in his mouth and gliding his tongue over it. When he was finished with one dark chocolate nipple, he gave the other equal attention.

Shari writhed, tilting her hips upward. She was drunk with the sensation of having his mouth on her.

Grant's fingertips trailed down her breasts to her flat stomach and then lower to her thighs and calves. He teased the tender spot at the underside of her knees before urging her legs apart with one knee.

He lingered at the curls between her thighs, palming her softly. Shari sucked in a deep breath when Grant thrust his finger inside her and stroked her gently. His finger eased out, then in, then out, then in again. It was such delicious torture that Shari didn't even realize Grant had changed his position until she felt his tongue inside her. His tongue flickered back and forth, deeper and deeper, higher and higher. Her orgasm was just out of reach and she thrust her hips forward.

"Oh, oh, oh," she gasped. Did his thumb feel better or his tongue? she wondered. She didn't know or care because after another thrust of his tongue on her clitoris, stars exploded behind her eyes, sending her into oblivion.

He returned to nuzzle her neck and she could feel him pulsing with desire against her thigh. "I need to be inside you," he murmured.

"Not yet," she said, once she'd recovered. She pulled herself up and laid one palm on his shoulder and another on his biceps. She lazily stroked his hard chest, and then she lowered her head and licked his nipples, gently biting them with her teeth. His eyes flickered open and then shut.

"Shari." He made a low, savage sound.

Shari smiled. She hadn't remembered that his nipples were a sensitive spot for him. Of course, the first time they'd made love she'd been somewhat intoxicated. But this time she wasn't intoxicated by liquor, only with thoughts of Grant.

While her mouth made a meal of his nipples, she slid one hand lower until she closed around his hard, masculine length. He throbbed and pulsed against her hand. She stroked the length of him again and again and he jerked in her hand.

"Shari, I need you now."

"What are you waiting for?"

Grant flipped Shari over until she was flat on her back and settled his erection at the juncture between her thighs. Grant was deliciously hot, sinfully sexy and the world fell away as he looked into her eyes. "Make love to me," she whispered.

Tender, yet demanding, Grant slid inside her. Her body, her hips and a place deep inside her that hadn't been touched in years sprang to life. He was so thick; it felt like he was rooted inside her. It scared Shari and she shut her eyes, arched her back and bent her knees so she could focus on the moment. Each thrust caused their bodies to go in a primal rhythm and the friction was so incredible, Shari thought she might die from happiness.

Grant seemed to understand her need because he didn't stop. Instead, he thrust harder, deeper, higher. It was so maddening, so disabling…she lost all choice or thought but staying in this moment with him. She squirmed underneath him, clenching her inner muscles as she took him more and more inside her.

Her breathing became rapid as he took her higher. In, out, in, out.

"Come with me." Grant moaned just as an intense orgasm, a wave of perfection, went through Shari and she went limp. Grant followed her as tremors shook his entire body and he collapsed on top of her.

The next morning, Shari was the first to wake up and a wicked smile spread across her face when she looked down at her husband who was sleeping soundly, but then just as a quickly a frown followed it.

The ramifications of being with Grant were far more potent than she could have ever imagined. He'd given and taken everything simultaneously, and all her defenses were down. Shari couldn't deny anymore that she was in love with her husband; she probably always had been. The way they'd made love last night had confirmed that. Grant had satisfied her like no other man had. He was an athletic and creative lover who'd been intent on ensuring her pleasure.

She was ready for them to have a real marriage, but was Grant? Was last night merely her being a convenient body next to him? He was a man, after all, with needs. What if last night was just sex to him? Shari wasn't sure how she would handle it, but on the other hand, if sex was the only way she could be close to her husband, to build a bond, then she would try anything. She wanted Grant to love her back as she loved him. The question was whether he could ever forgive her for keeping the truth about Andre from him, long enough to let love in?

As if reading her mind, Grant stirred in his sleep and then his eyes popped open. He didn't seem surprised to find Shari staring down at him. "Good morning," he murmured, wiping the sleep from his eyes.

Shari hoped Grant didn't regret their lovemaking last night. She got her answer when Grant reached for her, curled one hand around her neck and pulled her down on top of him so his mouth could charter every inch of her lips. His tongue pressed for entrance and Shari opened up to him and Grant dove inside, sweeping his tongue back and forth across hers. His fingertips trailed down her spine and then her ribs, waist and hips before his palm cupped her backside and brought her squarely against his erection.

"Well, good morning to you, too," she said as he nudged her legs apart, using his finger to tease her at the apex of her thighs to make sure she was wet and ready for him.

Shari enjoyed his tender touch and was ready to have him, hot and thick, inside her. She lifted her hips and Grant thrust strongly and Shari took him in deep.

Grant groaned and he tugged at her hair so she would open her eyes and look at him as they made love. He buried himself deep inside her over and over and Shari ground herself against him, rocking her hips back and forth.

"Easy, love," Grant said, slowing his movements and forcing her to maintain his pace. He seemed to want to delay them both from coming, to make the moment last longer. His palm on the small of her back guided her into a slow, rolling rhythm. Shari arched and her hips bucked upward. She wanted it harder. Faster. She wanted to be possessed by him. To go higher and higher.

"Shari, baby, oh, yes!" Grant's green eyes were dilated. His nostrils flared. His face flushed. He slipped his hands between them where they were joined together and Shari gasped.

Shari tightened her legs around his hips as the pressure of his probing fingers tantalized and teased her before sending her spiraling out of control. She came hard as wave after wave of contractions washed over her and everything around her fragmented into tiny little pieces.

Grant shuddered under her and gave a low, soft growl as his orgasm rippled through him.

Afterward, they lay together, bodies entwined, exhausted yet fully sated. Shari was unable to speak. She'd been unprepared for the ferocity of Grant's lovemaking this morning and unequipped to handle the love she now felt for her husband.

## Chapter 9

Grant leaned back in the bed, reviewing the night's and morning's events. Shari had long since gone to find out if she would be needed for the competition that day.

Last night, he'd thought he'd needed to comfort Shari because she'd been upset about running into his ex-wife, Dina, and he doubted that reunion was pleasant. He'd wanted her to feel wanted and he'd certainly done that, judging by the number of times she'd come.

And that's all he'd wanted to do last night—comfort her—but this morning…this morning had been different. He'd consciously set about bedding his wife. He'd woken up to find her naked beside him and staring down at him. His mouth had watered, and the need to taste her had grown stronger. She'd tasted like the closest thing to heaven, and he'd had to have another taste.

He was startled by his reaction to Shari. He'd known

he was attracted to her but maybe he'd been thinking of the young girl he'd had sex with in college. He'd been wrong. Shari was a grown woman now and they'd had take-no-prisoners sex last night, which probably had their hotel neighbors wishing they'd kept it down. Shari was so honest with her emotions and had let him know she'd enjoyed everything he'd done to her. She'd been vulnerable and had opened herself up to him, and he'd taken everything she had to offer.

He was in dangerous territory. There was still a lot unresolved between them and perhaps more on his side, but despite all of it, Grant knew that this morning would not be the last time he'd make love to Shari. He couldn't wait for later tonight when he would again have Shari screaming out his name as he was planted deep inside her.

Shari arrived at the studio glowing. Any doubts she'd had about making her marriage work had been eradicated when Grant had woken to make love to her again. She felt so satiated that even the sight of Dina in the kitchen dressed in fashionable skinny black jeans, a fitted red lace peplum top and chunky sandals could not sour her mood.

"Good morning," Shari said, breezing over to the Drayson family, who were in a corner discussing their plan of attack.

"Well, look who decided to join us," Drake replied when she joined the group.

"Good morning, cuz." Shari leaned over to give Drake a kiss on the cheek. Afterward, he gave her a bizarre look.

"Are you feeling okay?" Drake asked.

Usually when he razzed her, she got all upset, but not this morning.

"Yeah, what gives?" Belinda asked, eyeing her suspiciously.

Carter came forward and wrapped an arm around Shari's shoulders. "Did you guys forget that Shari here is a newlywed?"

Shari blushed knowingly. "Carter!"

Carter laughed. "Need I say more?" He released her out of his grasp.

Belinda immediately rushed over, grabbed Shari's hand and led her away from the family. "Did you and Grant, you know, get busy?"

Shari slapped her hand away. "Belinda. We are married."

"I know, but you guys got married so quickly and I just assumed you were doing it for Andre."

"Partly," Shari confirmed, "but as I told you weeks ago, Grant and I are rekindling our romance. Why aren't you happy for me?"

"I am, but this marriage was sudden, Shari, and I don't want you to get hurt."

"Well, you don't have to worry about that. I'm doing everything in my power to make my marriage work."

"Okay. And Grant?" Belinda asked, glancing at Shari. "Does he feel as you do? Is he putting his all into this marriage?"

Shari sighed. She didn't want to hear any negativity from Belinda. Not this morning. She wanted to bask in her lovemaking afterglow, and she refused to let Belinda change her positive outlook. "Gosh, Belinda, you sure know how to be a buzz-kill. I came here to see if you guys needed my help."

It turned out the family didn't. They had already decided to let Drake, Belinda and Malik go up in the next round against the other four competitors.

"So you don't need me here?" Shari asked, excitedly.

"Why, do you have some place you'd rather be, sis?" Monica inquired.

"Well…" Shari felt terrible for wanting to abandon the family, considering they'd all stuck around during her battle round yesterday, but she couldn't resist a chance to sneak away to spend more time with Grant. "Actually, I do. Grant is taking Andre to Disneyland and if you don't really need me, I can join them."

"Then you should go," Grandma Lillian said, coming forward to take both of Shari's hands. "Experience my great-grandson's first time at Disneyland. We have everything covered today, but we will need you back tomorrow."

"Are you sure, Grandma?" Shari asked.

"Absolutely. And as Carter mentioned earlier, this is your honeymoon, so go enjoy yourself with your family. Lillian's will take this next round."

"I agree," her father, Dwight, said, suddenly beside her. "Thanks to our preparation the last few weeks, we're in good shape."

Shari smiled broadly. They didn't have to convince her any further. "Great! I'll see you all later." She waved on her way out the door. Shari couldn't get out of the studio fast enough. She immediately pulled her cell phone out of her hobo bag and dialed Grant.

"Hello," his smooth, sexy voice said from the other end of the line.

"Hi," Shari said shyly. "Are you still at the hotel?"

"Yeah, kind of got a late start this morning," Grant replied.

"Good. Because I'm on my way back," Shari said. "I won't be baking in this round, so I can join you and Andre at Disneyland."

"That's great! Andre's going to be psyched having both of us today."

"I'm taking a taxi, but I'll see you in thirty minutes."

Later, Shari was thrilled to spend the day with Grant and Andre at Disneyland. She'd never felt so happy, so content, so at peace. Throughout the day, Grant had grabbed her hand and they'd walked hand-in-hand with Andre down Main Street. And when they weren't holding hands, he was sneaking a kiss when Andre wasn't looking or openly admiring her underneath hooded lashes. Shari doubted she would ever tire of looking into his green eyes.

And Andre was having the time of his life. Seeing how happy Andre was made Shari feel that the long day was well worth it. Grant paid extra so they could have lunch with Disney characters. Thanks to him, Andre met Mickey and Minnie Mouse, Donald Duck and Goofy. Andre was bursting with excitement and could hardly contain his glee. Or perhaps it was the cotton candy and sugary drinks he'd inhaled? Shari usually watched Andre's diet with a careful eye, but they were at Disneyland and she'd relented and allowed him a few goodies.

"I can't wait to take you back to the hotel tonight," Grant whispered in her ear, jolting Shari out of her daydream.

"Oh, yeah?"

"I can't wait to run my tongue down the length of your body and…" Grant whispered several naughty tidbits in her ear.

Shari not only blushed, but the place between her thighs began to feel warm at the thought of what Grant intended to do. He'd indicated he would take her to new heights.

And after they'd put an exhausted Andre to bed, Grant did just that. He gave her a knock-your-socks-off kiss that started when he lowered her onto the king-size bed of their master suite. He brushed his lips across hers and she eagerly parted her lips. Then his tongue touched hers and that's when the fun began. He sucked her tongue into his hot, moist cavern of a mouth and Shari's body revved into action. Her breath began to hitch and her heart thudded loudly in her chest. She wanted to sob with the pleasure of how his slow, deliberately deep kisses made her feel. He made love to her with his mouth while his hands slid around her hips to drag her back and forth against the rock-hard erection in his pants.

Shari had already known they were good together, but this meant more. They were making love because they wanted each other. And she wanted Grant something fierce. He had her throbbing, aching, panting and craving him. The past didn't exist between them anymore. There was no anger or resentment over lies and past hurts. It was just them living in the moment.

They strained together, arching their hips to be closer. Grant's thick length was nestled against her core, and Shari's nails clawed at his shirt, but it wasn't enough. They needed to touch each other.

"Let's get naked," Grant growled.

They both rose up slightly so Shari could tug his shirt over his head and Grant could ease her T-shirt over hers. He reached for the button on her jeans. One zip later, he was gliding his large, masculine hands over her hips and sliding the pants off her body. He struggled out of his jeans and boxers and they took the same route as hers and landed on a pile on the floor.

His erection was gloriously magnificent and Shari went to reach for him, but Grant didn't let her. Instead, he bent his head to skim his mouth across Shari's as he stroked her nipples underneath the satin bra she wore. Shari could feel her erect nipples stand up at attention. He reached behind her back to unlatch the bra and it fell to the bed. Grant's eyes grew large as he stared down at her round breasts and dark brown nipples.

Shari's fingers stroked his cheek and she could feel stubble from the day growing again, but she didn't care. She loved every part of this man. His beautiful green eyes, the dimple in his left cheek. This time, Shari initiated the kiss by grabbing both sides of Grant's face and falling backward onto the bed. She stroked her tongue over his lips until he opened his mouth. Her tongue darted inside, tangling with his. Grant's fingers plowed into her hair and pulled her closer, so he could taste her. Eventually, he left her lips and moved on to her cheeks, then her earlobes and then her neck. When he found the sensitive spot at the nape of her neck, he teased it, licking it gently at first and then sucking on it.

"What are you doing to me?" Shari struggled to control her emotions. She couldn't let him see how vulnerable she was, how raw. They were just figuring out what they were going to be to each other and what their mar-

riage would look like. She didn't want to ruin it by crying something out in the heat of the moment.

"Want me to stop?" he whispered in her ear, his
breathing deep and extreme. He continued to move
lower and lick her breasts. The way he worshipped
them, cupped them and sucked them into erect peaks
made Shari feel so beautiful. She didn't feel like a boring single mother. She felt alive. Womanly. Sexy.

Shari struggled to catch her breath, but finally managed to mutter, "No."

"Good. 'Cause I have more in store." Swiftly, Grant
tugged her bikini panties down her legs, tossing them
aside, and then returned to kiss her belly while his
hands roamed to her inner thigh. His fingers pried open
her outer lips and found her already wet for him. His
thumb skated over her clitoris in tiny little circles and
she shivered, her inner muscles clenching.

It felt so good that Shari moaned in pleasure.

Grant slid down the bed and Shari knew what was
coming next, but she wasn't prepared for the magnitude
of the passion Grant evoked in her. When he eased his
hand under her backside and pulled her closer to his
face, Shari held her breath in anticipation.

"So sweet, so sweet," Grant said seconds before his
tongue flicked across her clitoris. His first lick was slow
and gentle, but they became more urgent as he slowly
made his way deeper and deeper making figure eights
with his tongue.

Tiny eruptions began to course through her entire
body and Shari grabbed at the sheet as tension surged
through her.

But Grant didn't stop. He seemed intent on savoring
her and stoking the flame building inside her. An or-

gasmic cry escaped her lips as a tidal wave of pure ecstasy swept over her. Shari couldn't stand any more of his ministrations and grabbed Grant's head and pulled his mouth back toward her. Then she wrapped her ankles around his waist and arched her pelvis against him. A silent plea for him to take her and that she was prepared to receive him.

Grant growled low in his throat, then plunged inside her hard and deep. "You…feel…so good….Shari."

He lazily stroked Shari into oblivion with his lingering thrusts while kissing her greedily. She felt the heat and the pressure build. It was even more intoxicating when Grant put two fingers in her mouth. Shari sucked them feverishly as they moved together as one unit. He plunged into her with a steady cadence. Shari spread her legs wide and arched to meet his every thrust. Grant quickened above her one final time and they simultaneously soared into space and plummeted into a free fall back to earth.

"Grant, you have to let me up," Shari said the next morning when she tried unsuccessfully to push her husband's muscled arm from her torso.

"No, I want you to stay in bed with me." Grant's eyes were lit with lustful amusement.

"I can't. I'm in the bake-off today." Shari had kept an eye on her phone throughout yesterday and had seen the text from Belinda and then from her father and Carter telling her Lillian's had advanced to the third round. She had no idea what country *You Take the Cake* had in mind next, but she was needed back on set for Round 3.

"Can we come visit you today?" Grant asked, removing his arm and watching Shari rise from the bed.

"Andre has been dying to see what all the fuss is about and I think he might combust."

Uneasiness lurched in Shari's belly; she wasn't particularly thrilled with the aspect of Grant and Andre coming to the studio because Dina would be there. When had Grant and Dina seen each other last? She didn't want Dina anywhere near Andre, but she also didn't want to look insecure to Grant.

Shari turned around with a half smile. "Of course you can. It'll be fun."

"You sure?" Grant asked. He tilted her chin to face him. "I know you need to focus."

"It's fine." Shari attempted another halfhearted smile in an effort to convince her husband. "Andre will love the studio. You guys can take a tour while we're baking."

A smile spread across Grant's sensuous lips. "Great!"

"I'm going to shower," Shari said, throwing off the covers and rising from the bed.

"Would you like some company?" Grant asked mischievously.

Shari winked. "Love some."

An hour later, she was downstairs in the hotel restaurant where her family was gathered for a powwow session. The table was full with empty plates from the breakfast buffet. Shari had missed breakfast due to her late start.

"How was your day off with your family?" her father asked.

"Andre loved Disneyland. How did it go yesterday?"

"We annihilated the competition," Drake said. "They gave us the U.K. Belinda baked a Victoria sponge cake with a fresh berry compote and homemade whipped-cream filling that melted in your mouth. You should have seen the judges salivating."

Belinda smiled proudly at the compliment. "Thanks, Drake."

"What bakery was eliminated?" Shari asked.

"Double Yum Bakers."

"What country do you think is next?" Shari inquired. She was trying hard not to be jealous of the praise Belinda was receiving, but it was tough knowing that no matter how hard she tried, the family never seemed to pay much notice to what she could accomplish.

"Well, they haven't done Italy or the U.S. yet," Carter responded.

"Or they could try to throw us a curveball," Grandma Lillian added, "with something like Russia."

"I'm confident we can create a cake from any country," Carter replied.

"You sure are cocky when you have no idea what country they could pick, let alone what mystery ingredient," Drake said. "They could give you something like India or China, then what would you do?"

"Make it work!" Carter replied. "Because that's what I do. In case you hadn't noticed, I've been baking a tad bit longer than you."

"Now, now," Grandma Lillian admonished. "This competition is supposed to bring us together."

"And it will, Grandma," Drake replied. "It's just healthy competition between cousins."

"So who's doing this next round?" Shari asked. "Have you guys decided?"

"We are here just for moral support," Grandma Lillian replied, motioning to her husband and son

Dwight. "I want my grandchildren to rise to the occasion. They've decided this round will be you, Carter and Belinda."

"What about me?" Monica inquired. She'd been learning the ropes of the bakery the past couple of years and was starting to become a decent baker.

"Maybe next round, kid," Carter replied. "This competition is for the big boys."

Monica frowned at her older cousin. "I'm no child," Monica replied. "I want to bake in the next round."

"Of course you can," Grandma Lillian replied. "This is a *family* operation. And you would all do best to remember that." She looked around at all her grandchildren, paying particular attention to Carter.

Carter rolled his eyes upward, but didn't say anything more that might upset their grandmother. Matter of fact, she'd put everyone in their place and they'd all settled into a quiet silence and left the restaurant.

An hour later, the Drayson family, Brown Sugar Bakery, Delovely Cakemakers and Bliss were standing in front of Brandon, the host for *You Take the Cake*. "Are you guys ready for another round of cakes around the world?"

"Yes," the bakers said in unison as they assembled behind their stations complete with industrial-size mixers, large mixing bowls, spatulas and cake pans.

Shari was excited about the day and determined to show off her talents. The past couple of days, Carter and Belinda had really shined. Now it was time for Shari's place in the sun.

"Your country today is Italy," Brandon announced. "As in previous rounds, you'll be judged on presentation, taste and creativity. If everyone is ready, open your boxes to show your mystery ingredients. We'll be asking you to come up with a miniature-size cake that incorporates these ingredients while being true to Italy."

Shari reached for the box first and pulled out carob, avocado and salsa. "What the heck?" What were they supposed to do with salsa?

"Don't worry," Carter whispered in her ear. "I've got an idea."

Shari, Carter and Belinda huddled together for several minutes and once they had a plan formulated, they went into action. Carter went about making a *Buccellato,* an Italian cake synonymous with Sicily, and would incorporate a savory salsa. Shari went for the avocado, so she could show her range of baking.

Belinda gave her a raised brow as if she was surprised Shari didn't go for the safe choice—the carob, which was a healthy form of chocolate. "I'm going to make a killer Tiramisu," Belinda told Shari.

"That's great." Shari ignored her cousin and proceeded to prepare her avocado cake with a sunflower-butter-cream frosting.

After they completed the first challenge, Shari, Carter and Belinda watched as the judges sampled their creations. The judges praised the texture of Belinda's carob tiramisu. When the judges came to her avocado cake, Shari's heart leaped in her throat.

"Very nice," the judge said. "Just the right amount of avocado. It doesn't overpower the cake. It's light and airy. Delicious."

"Thank you." Shari smiled and glanced at Carter.

And then her heart deflated almost immediately when another judge added, "Although it was moist and delicious, I would have loved to have seen some candied sunflowers on the top for that added crunch."

Shari nodded, but didn't say a word.

She was nervous when they reached for Carter's miniature *Buccellato*. Though it was typically made with honey, Marsala and raisins, Carter had switched out the Marsala for savory salsa.

"Inventive," the judges both proclaimed. "A very creative way to use the mystery ingredient. I'm impressed. I might have to steal the recipe for myself."

Shari's heart sank. Despite her good showing, her cousins still managed to outshine her. Shari plastered a smile on her face as Carter's and Belinda's work would ensure Lillian's continued to the next round.

After their critiques, they had a thirty-minute break before the next challenge of making a traditional Italian wedding cake large enough to feed two hundred guests. They decided to go with thick cream cheese frosting over a decadent white cake infused with coconut.

Shari stepped away from the kitchen studio for a much-needed break. The judge's critique upset her and deep down she knew why. She was letting her insecurities about her baking skills and her place at Lillian's define her. She would have to stop yielding to her cousins at every turn and take the lead. But how could she when she was always so used to letting them win?

# *Chapter 10*

From the other side of the room, Grant watched as Shari walked off the set. He'd just walked in with Andre so he could see Shari in action for himself. The judges had given Lillian's an enthusiastic thumbs-up for all their creations. The other teams had fared pretty well, including Brown Sugar Bakery, whose *cassata* and *panettone* had won equally good praise. He was about to come forward when he saw Shari leave the studio. On stage, he noticed that her smile seemed forced and didn't completely reach her eyes.

The more time he spent with Shari, the more he was able to discern her moods. She was upset, but why? Lillian's was obviously doing well.

Andre tugged on his hand. Grant looked down at his son.

"Can I go on set, Daddy?" Andre inquired.

"Sure, just let me find your mommy first," Grant said. As he looked around, he noticed his ex-wife sashaying toward him.

He frowned. This was not a reunion he wanted to have right now. He needed to find Shari and find out what was wrong. He stepped to the right to move past Dina, but she didn't budge.

"Grant." Dina inclined her head.

"Dina." He hadn't seen his ex-wife since that day in court when they'd both agreed to a divorce and signed the papers. His parents hadn't been happy about his failed marriage but Grant couldn't care less. He should never have married Dina to begin with.

"Is this your son?" Dina asked, bending down until she was Andre's height. She stared at the young boy in a red polo shirt and blue jean shorts. "Of course he is. With those green eyes and dimples, he looks just like you."

Grant leaned down and whispered to Andre. "You see your grandma in the corner?"

Andre nodded.

"Go sit with her until I'm finished, okay?"

"Okay, Daddy."

Grant watched Andre walk across the stage until he was safely in his grandmother's arms. He noticed that Lillian Reynolds-Drayson gave him a long glare once she saw who he was talking to.

He turned to face Dina. "What do you want?"

"Is that how you greet your ex-wife who you haven't seen in years?" She leaned into him for a hug, but Grant stepped backward.

"It's how I treat someone who lied to me," Grant responded, stepping away from the cameras and moving into the corner of the stage.

"Lied to you?"

"Oh, c'mon, Dina." Grant gave her a sardonic glare. "Don't play dumb. I know what you did five years ago."

Dina stared behind Grant at his son. "Do you mean your son? Because if you're saying that I knew Shari was pregnant, then you're wrong. I had no idea."

Grant couldn't believe Dina's nerve. "You're actually going to stand there and lie to my face after you've been caught? You were her roommate, Dina. Of course you knew. But you had an agenda and you weren't going to let my child get in your way."

Dina shook her head fervently. "That's not true. And I told Shari the same thing."

"Really? And you would have stepped aside had you known? I don't think so. You made sure I thought Shari was off-limits by telling me that she was engaged to that Thomas guy. You deliberately misled me. Why should I believe that you didn't go so far as to keep me from my child?"

"I would *never* do that."

"So you say, Dina. So you say. Did you even love me at all?" Despite himself, Grant's voice rose. "Or was I just a challenge for you to steal away from Shari?"

Grant didn't notice that *You Take the Cake's* producer, a large, lanky fellow with spectacles, was standing a few yards from him and Dina trying to look inconspicuous as he listened to their conversation. Nor did he see Shari who'd returned from taking a breath of fresh air, standing behind the curtain.

"Why do the two of you want to rewrite history and act like I kept two lovebirds apart?" Dina asked bitterly.

"Because we both know that's a lie, Grant. You liked what I had to offer." She glided her hands down her side. "The beauty, the brains... Matter of fact—" she paused, bringing her index finger to her mouth "—I recall you couldn't get enough of me." She circled around him. "Or had you forgotten that fact?"

"That isn't what this is about, Dina," Grant said, his face turning red at Dina's boldness. "It's about your lies and deception about Shari."

"Shari? You had a one-night stand with her, which was nothing more than a cheap hookup and she happened to get pregnant. You two had nothing in common. She was a mousy undergrad who was afraid of her own shadow back then. Hell, she still is. She's so afraid of never being good enough. She can't even take the heat in the kitchen." Dina pointed to the studio kitchen. "Don't go blaming me because you jumped out of her bed into mine. You're the reason you missed out on your son's life, not me."

Dina stormed away from Grant.

Grant stared at her retreating figure. Dina had a point. He had made the stupid decision of getting involved with Dina so soon after his night with Shari. Of course Shari would be upset that he'd hooked up with her best friend. He *was* partially to blame, but he wasn't alone. Dina had ensured he would not pursue Shari by lying to him about Shari's relationship with Thomas, thereby ensuring he'd run into her arms.

Grant wanted to go after Dina and tell her another thing or two, but when he looked up, he noticed they'd had an audience. Several members of the crew were standing nearby. How long had they been there? Grant didn't want to cause another scene and chose not to go after Dina. Instead, he walked over to Lillian.

"Everything okay?" she asked, playing with Andre and his action figures.

"Everything's fine," Grant said curtly. Or it would be. He owed Shari an apology. He'd put all the blame on her and Dina for lying and keeping the truth from him when he wasn't completely blameless, either. They'd all contributed to Andre growing up without him. But that would never happen again. He was determined more than ever to make his marriage to Shari work.

"Did you see the fireworks between that man and Dina English, the owner of Brown Sugar Bakery?" the producer asked Drew, the director of *You Take the Cake*.

"I did hear raised voices, but I was a little preoccupied."

"I think there's a gold mine here," the producer said. "There's some tension between Lillian's and Brown Sugar Bakery. I want you to keep an eye on them for the rest of the competition."

"You do realize this is a baking competition not a reality show?" Drew asked, a bit miffed by the producer's instructions.

"Yes, but ratings are the most important thing," the producer responded. "So you focus on the personal interaction between the competitors and let me figure out how we capitalize on it. *Capisce?*"

The director nodded reluctantly.

From behind the curtain, Shari wiped the tears from her eyes with the back of her hand. Grant hadn't stood up for her to Dina. She'd hoped after the last few days that they'd spent together in Los Angeles that he was starting to care for her. Was she imagining the whole thing? She had to be because he'd let Dina rail on her. He hadn't defended her when Dina called her mousy and afraid of her own shadow.

The words still stung. Even after all these years, Dina could still cut her like a knife. Shari had thought time and distance would lessen the pain she'd felt by her former friend's betrayal, but seeing her day after day was bringing up every insecurity Shari had ever had about herself. Added to the fact that she was fighting with her cousins for the chance to run Lillian's and it was just too much. Shari was reaching her breaking point.

She'd tried so hard in the competition to show she was as good a baker as Carter or Belinda, but she always came up short. Even the judges today had praised Carter's creation as innovative, while she got *very nice.*

Just then, her iPhone rang, but she didn't recognize the number. "Hello?"

"Who is this?" a woman's voice said testily from the other end of the line.

"Excuse me?"

"Why are you answering my son's phone?" the woman pressed.

Shari looked down at the phone again and noticed that she must have grabbed Grant's phone by mistake. She raised the phone back to her ear.

"This is Shari."

"And, I'm asking again, who are you?"

Shari was fed up with being bullied, especially today of all days. "This is Grant's wife. Who is this?"

Silence ensued on the other line for several long moments before the woman cleared her voice. "Did you say *wife?*"

"Yes, I'm Shari Robinson, the mother of Grant's child," Shari added for good measure. She figured the woman on the other end was one of his bevy of beauties from New York, and she'd had enough of people walking over her.

"Oh!"

Shari could hear the surprise in the woman's voice.

"I…I'm Grant's mother, Eleanor Robinson," the woman said awkwardly on the other end of line. "And I guess I'm going to be a grandmother."

Shari swallowed hard. She'd had no idea that the woman was Grant's mother. His caller ID hadn't said Mom or Mother. It had merely had her name: Eleanor. "I'm…so…so sorry, Mrs. Robinson." Words began spilling out of Shari's mouth. "I had no idea."

"The same can be said for me," Grant's mother replied. "I had no idea that Grant was married, much less going to be a father. How far along are you?"

Shari sighed. Of course Mrs. Robinson would think she was pregnant. She would never assume she had a four-year-old grandchild. "Umm…" Shari stammered, unclear of how to proceed. "I'm not pregnant."

"You're not? Then what did you mean you're the mother of his child?"

Shari was sure that Grant would have preferred to tell his parents himself and now she'd opened the proverbial Pandora's Box. There was no going back now. She just had to spit it out and let the chips fall where they may. Grant should have told them by now, anyway. "Our son, Andre, is four years old," she finally said.

"Oh!" She heard his mother's loud exclamation.

"How can this be? Grant never told us. I mean, I know we're not close and we've been estranged for years, but to keep our grandson from us? It's beyond comprehension."

Shari heard the announcer say that she was due back on set. "I'm sorry, Mrs. Robinson, but I can't go into more detail. I really have to go. Perhaps we can talk later?"

"We're in Los Angeles," Mrs. Robinson said. "We won't be back East for several days."

Shari nodded, recalling Grant had mentioned his parents were on a Mexican Riviera cruise. "So are we," Shari responded. "How about dinner at 7:00 p.m.? You can meet us at our hotel."

"Oh, my goodness," Mrs. Robinson responded. "I would like that. I can't wait to meet my grandson." And then she added as an afterthought, "And you as well, my dear."

"See you tonight." Shari rattled off the hotel's address before ending the call. In the back of her mind, Shari knew she'd been somewhat vindictive. She hadn't had to tell his mother who she was or about Andre. She merely could have said that she'd have Grant call her back. Perhaps if he'd told them sooner, she wouldn't have had to blindside his mother. Grant was not going to be happy that she'd gotten his parents involved in their drama, but there was no way around it.

Shari didn't have time to tell Grant what occurred or to give Andre a kiss because she had to get back on set. She continued the rest of the competition and Lillian's Bakery came out on top along with Brown Sugar Bakery and Delovely Cakemakers. Two more days of competition left and they'd be done. Then it would be back to Chicago...and to what?

Shari wasn't sure where she stood in her marriage. Sure, she knew that she and Grant were great together in the bedroom. It was out of the bedroom that they had a problem.

She found Grant and Andre waiting for her after she'd cleaned up. "Hi, guys." Shari forced herself to smile even though she felt the exact opposite.

"Hey, babe." Grant leaned down and pressed a kiss against her lips. He lifted her face up when he noticed Shari didn't respond to his kiss. "Tough day?"

"Something like that," Shari responded curtly as she looked away.

"Where are we going tonight, Mommy?"

"I'm not sure, sweetie pie," Shari said. "I think we might actually have some company at dinner."

"Oh, yeah?" Grant lifted a brow. "Are the Draysons having another family dinner tonight?"

Shari's eyes darted nervously back and forth. She was afraid to look at Grant directly. "No, the Robinsons."

"Excuse me?"

She raised her eyes to find his green ones boring into her. "Your parents are in town and are meeting us for dinner."

"I'm going to meet Daddy's parents?" Andre asked from her side. He started jumping up and down with excitement.

Shari glanced at Grant again and noticed that fury was emanating out of every pore, and that he was trying with great difficulty to keep himself in check in front of Andre. His eyes, however, told Shari that she misstepped gravely, but she was through living in the shadows. "That's right. So let's go back to the hotel and get changed. How does that sound?"

Shari headed for the door. She didn't wait to see if Grant was behind her.

Once at the hotel, she gave Andre the longest bath known to man before finally getting him dressed and letting him watch a cartoon. She entered the master suite to shower and Grant was waiting for her.

He was already dressed in tailored slacks, a pale green silk shirt and loafers. Any other man wouldn't be able to wear a pastel color, but it brought out the brilliant color of Grant's eyes and made him even more handsome.

"What the hell were you thinking?" He jerked to his feet from the bed. "You had no right."

"I had every right," Shari said fiercely. "You should have told them about me and Andre."

"I didn't want to disrupt their trip."

"Excuses, excuses. Would there have ever been a right time, Grant? Or were you just going to keep them in the dark and keep Andre and me a secret forever?"

Grant turned around, surprised. "Is that really what you think after our time together here?"

"What am I supposed to think?" Shari asked, regarding him warily. "You didn't invite them to the wedding."

"There's a lot you don't understand, Shari."

"Of course there is," Shari said, sweeping past him into the master bath and slamming the door. None of which Grant seemed willing to share with her. He was willing to share his body with her, but his feelings, his hurts, his pains, those were strictly off-limits.

She emerged half an hour later, showered and fully

dressed in a simple one-shoulder pleated dress in navy blue that stopped at her knee. She'd curled her long hair loosely, so it hung in soft waves down her back. She'd agonized about her makeup until finally deciding to be herself and keep it simple—a few brushes of mineral foundation, a touch of mascara and lipstick and she was set. Simple gold hoop earrings adorned her ears and a diamond and gold necklace, a gift for her twenty-first birthday from her father, circled her neck.

"You look beautiful," Grant said when he saw her.

Given his previous anger at her, she was surprised by the begrudging compliment. "Thank you."

"Listen," Grant began, but a knock sounded on the door to their suite. Grant glanced at the door. "We'll talk later." He walked toward the door and paused for several seconds before opening it.

"Grant!" His mother, a tall, slender woman, stepped into the doorway. "You're looking well, dear."

"Yes, Grant, you are looking good." His father shook his hand, but didn't hug him.

"Thanks, Pops."

Shari waited for Grant to introduce her, but the Robinsons seemed to be struggling for how to continue until she stepped forward.

"Oh, yes," Grant said as if forgetting his manners, "this is my wife, Shari Robinson. Shari, my parents, Eleanor and Warren."

Shari stepped forward to meet them. "It's a pleasure to meet you, Mr. and Mrs. Robinson."

"I wish I could say the same, dear, but all this comes as quite a shock to us," Grant's mother pronounced. "We have a grandson we know nothing about, a rushed marriage, which we weren't even invited to. Do you have anything to say for yourself?"

"Mother, it's not Shari you're upset with," Grant said, stepping in between the two women. "It's me. I'm the one who chose to keep our wedding ceremony small."

"Without your parents?" She huffed, turning around to glare at him. "First that Dina woman and now this!" His mother threw her hands up in the air and walked away. Shari watched her head toward the minibar that had been set up in the room. She went about making herself a gin and tonic.

"Eleanor, really, must you be so dramatic?" Grant's father said. "Shari." He came toward her and held out his hand. "Welcome to the family."

Shari found the offer of a handshake somewhat formal and instead leaned forward to hug her father-in-law. She noticed him stiffen ever so slightly before giving her a quick pat and pulling away. Did the Robinsons not hug each other?

"Where is my grandson?" Mr. Robinson inquired, looking around the suite. "And what's his name?"

"Andre." Grant beat Shari to the punch. "His name is Andre and he's the most amazing four-year-old you're ever going to meet. He's bright and funny."

"Just like you were," his mother said from the couch where she'd plopped herself with her drink.

"I'll go get him," Shari said, and rushed into the adjoining room where Andre was watching a cartoon. She was eager for a few minutes to herself to figure out exactly what was going on out there. Grant's parents were cold and distant. They weren't remotely like Grant, who was warm and affectionate. Was that how he'd grown up? Was that why he'd chosen to keep Shari and Andre away from them?

"Hey, honey," Shari said, coming beside Andre to join him on the queen-size bed in his room. He wasn't used to having such a big bed all to himself. He'd tried to sneak in their bed last night when Shari and Grant were naked underneath the covers. She'd had to ask Andre to turn his head while she'd slid on a robe. Then she'd put him back in his own bed and stayed with him until he'd fallen asleep. She loved watching Andre sleep. Listening to his soft snoring. Touching his dimpled cheek. "You ready to meet your grandparents?"

"Are they here?" Andre asked, jumping off the bed. Before she could stop him, Andre was rushing out of the bedroom and into the master suite.

"Grandpa!" Andre went rushing toward Mr. Robinson. Shari thought he would shun her son's wild display of affection, but instead, something must have clicked in his head, because he scooped him up into his arms and gave him a hug.

When Shari glanced in her father-in-law's direction, tears shone in his eyes. "He looks just like you, son," he said, looking directly at Grant. "He's your spitting image."

"I know." Grant smiled broadly for the first time since his parents' arrival. It was clear he couldn't be more proud of Andre.

Andre wiggled in his grandfather's arms, eager to be put down on the floor. When he was, he rushed over to greet Eleanor Robinson. "Grandma!"

She seemed surprised to hear him speak to her and she looked up at him strangely from the bottom of her drink. "I am."

"I already have a grandma," Andre replied, "but you can be my nana. Is that okay?"

Speechless, Eleanor looked up at Grant and then her husband. "That would be fine."

"Good." Andre jumped into her lap and when he did, the tumbler in her hand shook, spilling liquid onto her Chanel suit. "I'm sorry, Nana." He looked up at Shari, waiting to be scolded.

Shari clutched her chest, horrified by Andre's actions, and rushed to the minibar to find some seltzer water. When she found some, she rushed with a nearby linen napkin to Eleanor's side. Given the Robinsons' stiff nature, she didn't know how Eleanor was going to react, but instead of scolding Andre, she chuckled. "Don't worry. Nana shouldn't have been drinking it, anyway."

Eleanor placed the tumbler on the cocktail table adjacent to the sofa. She accepted the napkin Shari offered and blotted her lap.

"How about dinner?" Grant asked from behind them.

Shari nodded. "That sounds like a good idea."

## Chapter 11

Hours later, the Robinson family returned to their hotel suite. They had gone to a famous Italian eatery where Shari watched Andre make a mess of his spaghetti and meatballs in front of Eleanor and Warren Robinson. She'd been surprised at how Grant's parents had finally warmed up after their initial cold reception. They'd even stopped in the hotel gift shop to buy a toy for Andre before departing.

After all the excitement of the evening and his bath, Andre went out like a light. Shari tucked Andre underneath the covers, turned out the lamp by his nightstand and rose to leave. That's when she saw Grant standing in the doorway.

"I'd like to talk to you, Shari."

"Does it have to be tonight? It's been a really long day." She attempted to scoot past him in the doorway, but his large masculine frame didn't move.

"Yes, it does," Grant said. Grasping her by the arm, he pulled her out of Andre's room and closed the door. When they were back in the master bedroom, he let her have it. "What the hell were you thinking, bringing my parents into this?"

"They had a right to know they have a grandson."

"It was my place to tell them, not yours."

"Maybe so." Shari shrugged, conceding the point. "But when? Were you ever going to tell them? Or perhaps you were going to wait until Andre started high school?"

"Not funny, Shari." His voice hardened.

"I didn't think it was."

"Then you should have stayed out of my family's business."

Shari whirled around. "Wait a second. I thought Andre and I were your family or at least that's what you touted when you forced me into marrying you. Give Andre a loving two-parent home, you said." She laughed derisively. "As if you would know what one feels like. Your parents are as cold as ice."

The minute she said the words, Shari knew she'd gone too far. She'd hit Grant below the belt and the stormy look on his face confirmed it. He stalked toward her. "You don't know the first thing about my family. You, who were raised a Drayson. You guys are joined at the hip. You live together. You work together. What would you know about a dysfunctional family like mine?"

Shari was surprised to hear him admit that all was not right with the Robinson family. She'd caught a hint of their ambivalence when Eleanor Robinson had immediately reached for a drink upon her arrival, but that didn't stop Shari from retaliating now and responding to Grant's harsh words. "I know plenty. I know what it's like being the dimly lit star in the family. Always having your cousins or siblings outshine you. Being pitted against them in the quest to be on top at Lillian's Bakery. We may seem like the perfect family, but we can be just as dysfunctional, Grant Robinson."

Grant stared back at her. He understood now what he'd seen at the studio earlier when she'd run out after the judges had congratulated Carter on a job well-done. "So we have something in common."

"If you could call it that," she muttered underneath her breath.

"Then why did you call my parents?" Grant asked, walking toward her. "You did this on purpose to get a rise out of me, didn't you?"

"So what if I did?" Shari lowered her lashes, somewhat embarrassed by her actions, because she had told his mother to be spiteful. "You were sweeping our marriage under the rug as if I wasn't important."

Shari didn't realize that Grant had closed the distance between them until he was inches away from her face. "And you want to be front and center in my world?"

Shari's breath caught in her throat when she saw the hungry gaze in Grant's eyes. She knew that look because he'd had it each and every time he'd made love to her, each and every time he'd made her come over and over and over again.

Grant peeled off his jacket, yanked at the knot of his tie until it loosened and then shrugged out of his shirt. When he did, he revealed a broad chest that looked as if it had been chiseled with a hammer. His stomach was lean and Shari saw just enough of his six-pack abs before they disappeared into his pants.

"I do," she murmured, studying him, drinking him in. He was perfect in every detail.

"Then by all means, let me show you that you are." He rushed toward her to kiss her open-mouthed. His tongue sought hers with desperate need. In an instant he was lifting her off the ground and backing her up against the wall. She wrapped her legs around his hips so she could grind herself against his bulging erection. The friction was building in steady waves. Grant began unzipping the back of her dress while he stroked her long and deep with her tongue. She didn't notice her dress fall to her waist because Grant was nipping at her jaw. At her chin. At her ear. Then her breasts as he pushed up her bra.

His tongue grazed her nipple. He teased, licked and sucked on the bud until it puckered for him. And then he began devouring it like he was a newborn babe. Shari bit back a scream, for fear Andre would hear her. She'd never seen Grant so take-charge and a little out of control, but never once did she stop him. When his hands fanned the spheres of her buttocks, cupping them, Shari moaned, urging him on.

Grant continued his quest by using his fingers to trace up the edge of her inner thigh and Shari stopped breathing. He paused there for seconds before he moved aside the fabric of her panties and slid his finger inside her. He made circular motions with his finger while his tongue duplicated the act in her mouth. In and out. In and out. A delighted gasp escaped from Shari's lips.

She heard the sound of Grant's pants buckle and a rush of air as his pants fell to the floor.

"You really want to be the center of my world?" Grant whispered.

"Yes...oh, yes." Panting, Shari leaned her head back against the wall as his finger circled inside of her. Her breath, ragged and tangled, began to catch in her throat. She wrapped her arms around Grant's neck, just as he removed his fingers and entered her.

Urgent and demanding, he thrust his hips upward into her and gripped her behind to keep her from falling. He drove into her again and again. Shari undulated up and down against him, lost in fantasy and in reality, she didn't know which. Soon her orgasm was coiling within her and her nails dug into his back. Then she gave a silent scream into his neck as pure pleasure radiated through her.

Grant thrust one final time and then grunted before collapsing against her.

Once her muscles relaxed, the throbbing ebbed and her shallow breathing became normal again, Shari slid her quivering legs back onto the floor. She feared that if Grant let go of his grip on her that she'd dissolve into a pile of putty.

He held her with one strong, muscled arm against the wall and stroked her hair with his free hand. "Dear God, woman, what have you done to me?"

"Excuse me?" Shari asked, pushing aside the hair that had fallen down in her face and tucking it behind her ear. "You're the one that was a little frenzied."

Grant smiled as he looked down at his pants pooled around his ankles. He'd barely had time enough to unzip them before he'd taken her against the wall. Part anger, part lust, he'd wanted her. Fast and hard. And she hadn't disappointed. Shari was an enigma. At times sweet and fragile, and at other times bold and daring. He was beginning to like all facets of his wife.

"You didn't seem to have a problem with it," he said, pulling up his pants.

"You're not the only one that can be frenzied." Shari laughed wickedly and once she had her footing, pushed Grant toward the chaise in their suite.

"What are you doing?" Grant said, looking up at her as she removed her clothing that he'd unceremoniously pushed aside when he'd had his way with her.

When she was naked, she came toward him and removed his shoes first. Then his trousers and briefs until his hard throbbing member was naked to her eyes, to her lips.

Shari knelt to her knees and took Grant in her hands. His erection was taut and throbbing.

Grant watched her. His expression was tight and lustful as she slowly began to stroke him.

"I want to taste you," she said.

"Hurry," he groaned.

Shari smiled at him and then she lowered her head, curled both hands around his penis and licked the head.

A savage groan tore from Grant's throat. His hands slid into her hair, bunching it, clenching it. He saw her lips open seconds before she took him full and deep inside her wet mouth. She circled him with her tongue, using light, gentle flicks and then went deep again. While the warm suction of her mouth took him higher and higher, her hands were teasing him to distraction.

As she sucked him dry, she looked up at him with a steady gaze. His eyes met hers and his teeth clenched.

"Shari, I need you now." His voice was rough and thick with desire.

Shari obliged and rose to her feet but not before licking her lips as if he was the best meal she'd ever tasted. She spread her legs wide and then straddled him, taking him all the way inside her body. She was wet and tight and felt so good.

"Shari…it's…so…so good." Grant could barely get the words out.

Her body tightened unbearably around him and he could feel his penis flex inside her. That's when she started rocking her hips against him, undulating and grinding. It was driving him mad and he threw his head back, trying to keep his body from releasing. "You're making me lose control," he muttered.

When Shari slowed her actions, he said, "Don't stop!"

As much as her torturous strokes were sending him to the brink, he didn't want her to stop.

His fingers came up to skim her breasts. He squeezed the nipples, stroking and teasing them with the pads of his fingers. Shari cupped her breasts and offered her sensitive nipples to him as a gift.

"Yes, baby, lift those breasts to me," he groaned. She moaned out her pleasure when his mouth closed on one tightened peak, and he began sucking as he'd done earlier. He'd noticed she liked it and used the exact same pressure and suction.

She pushed her pelvis harder against him and Grant took the hint and reached down to stroke her clitoris where they were joined.

"Yes, oh, yes, like that," Shari said. "Touch me there." He felt her internal muscles clench around him and she shattered in his arms. Grant was right behind her and gave an exultant male cry as white-hot electricity shot straight through him.

Grant was already up when Shari awoke the next morning. She'd hoped to find him curled up next to her in bed as exhausted and sated as she was. Last night had been even more wonderful than their previous encounters. Her sexual attraction to Grant was visceral and powerful, and she'd completely given herself to him, but she still had no clue how he felt about her. He could show her in the way he kissed, touched her, made love to her, but he didn't speak the three little words her soul yearned to hear.

There was no mistaking that she was head over heels in love with Grant. When she was in his arms she felt like she belonged to him and that she mattered. Like she was home. It scared her to know that her feelings for Grant were that strong. What if he tired of her? They'd gotten married so suddenly, and after the initial glow wore off, after he'd built a relationship with Andre, he could want his freedom. He could want to end their marriage. The thought frightened Shari and she sat upright in the bed.

Grant walked in at that moment bare chested and wearing pajama bottoms and holding a tray. Then his focus changed and she noticed he wasn't looking her in the eye, but was staring at her chest. That's when Shari reached for the sheet to cover her breasts.

"Don't." Grant smiled coming forward. He bent down to sweep his mouth over hers. "I like seeing you so free and uninhibited." Grant sat beside her and slid the tray with coffee, yogurt, fruit and toast on her lap.

Although that hadn't been her intention, Shari smiled nonetheless. She accepted the proffered tray. "Thank you."

"We worked up an appetite," Grant said. "I thought you might be hungry."

"I'm ravenous," Shari said, reaching for the wheat toast and taking a generous bite.

"I bet," Grant said. He grasped hold of the second coffee mug on the tray and sipped. "I didn't recognize you last night."

"Nor I, you."

"Well, I think emotions were a little high last night," Grant said. "We pushed each other's buttons."

Shari hazarded a glance in Grant's direction. She knew she was primarily at fault for the discord between them. She had informed his parents of their marriage without discussing it with him first. "I'm sorry. I shouldn't have butted my nose into your relationship with your parents."

"If you hadn't, I doubt I would have seen my parents look as happy as they did last night," Grant answered honestly. "You gave them a grandson."

"True, but that wasn't why I told them."

Grant turned to face her. "What was it about, then? Was it about competing with your cousins in the show?"

"I always come up short," Shari said, placing the tray on the nightstand. "Everyone asks for Carter's creations at the store, Belinda is beloved by Grandma. Drake has his niche with the social-media thing and his cookbook. Even though I came up with selling Lillian's baking mixes, I'm still undervalued."

"You are a wonderful mother," Grant interjected. "And a great baker. I've tasted some of your delicacies."

The apple tartlet she'd brought him from work in Chicago a couple of weeks ago had been divine. "Why do you give yourself so little credit?"

Shari blinked back the tears threatening to form. "This competition, seeing Dina again, battling for supremacy at Lillian's. It's been a lot."

"Including our rushed marriage?" Grant asked.

When Shari didn't answer right away, Grant reached for the phone sitting on the nightstand. Shari had no idea who he was calling, but then she heard him ask for Dwight Drayson's room. Then she heard him talking to a female who she assumed was her mother. "Yes, ma'am. I was hoping that if Shari wasn't in this round that we could spend the day together, just she and I. Do you think you would be able to watch Andre for us? You would? That's great. Thank you, Mrs. Drayson. Shari and I truly need some alone time. We'll call you later this afternoon. Okay, thanks."

When he turned back around to face her, Shari was in disbelief. Grant had just made arrangements with her mother to ensure that they would spend the whole day together, just the two of them. "Grant…" She was speechless and her voice caught in her throat.

"What?" He acted as if he was surprised by her reaction.

"You know what." Shari threw caution to the wind, tossed off the sheets and jumped naked into Grant's waiting arms. "You know exactly what I need."

Their day together was everything Shari could have hoped for. After making love again, they had showered and set about seeing more of Los Angeles. Their first stop was a tour of Warner Bros. studio where they would get a behind-the-scenes glance of how movies and TV shows were made at the studio.

Shari was excited as they waited at the Warner Bros. gift store for the tour to begin. Holding hands, she and Grant perused the merchandise while sipping on Starbucks coffee. Shari felt like a normal couple on vacation.

Their tour guide, EJ, took them around on a golf cart big enough to sit eight. Shari and Grant were squeezed together, but she didn't mind at all. She was having the time of her life. The guide was very knowledgeable as he took them around the back lot and sound stage. He explained the film processes and how the studio's set could be altered. Shari discovered Grant was quite the movie aficionado and asked lots of questions.

Halfway through their two-and-a-half-hour tour, they were able to walk on the set of a hit television series and browse through some of the costumes and props. They ended the tour by standing in front of a large green screen, which, thanks to Grant's fascination with Batman, had a bat backdrop.

"That was fun," Shari said once they were back in the rental car after the tour with their Batman photo in hand.

"You needed to let your hair down," Grant replied, starting the engine. "You know, have some fun. The Draysons have been taking this *You Take the Cake* competition way too seriously."

"If a member of my family heard you say that, it would be sacrilege."

"What if Lillian's doesn't win?" Grant inquired as he eased out of the parking lot and onto the highway.

Shari didn't hesitate with a response. "That's not an

option. Although she says otherwise, Grandma will accept nothing less than a win, especially going against Dina."

Grant nodded in understanding. "I just see what this competition and the rivalry between the two bakeries is doing to you."

"Being here with you is helping," Shari said, smiling in his direction.

"I'm glad," Grant said, offering her an irresistibly devastating grin, "but this tour wasn't all I have in store for you today."

"Oh, yeah? What's next?"

"You'll see."

They took a short drive to Long Beach marina. Shari was confused by their destination because she was not a boat woman. The only time she'd ever been on a boat was a family dinner cruise on the *Spirit of Chicago* on Lake Michigan. "Are we sailing?" she asked, looking apprehensively at the watercrafts.

"No, we're going on that." He pointed to the fleet of gondolas waiting down by the docks. "C'mon." Grant grasped her hand and led her to a white picket fence decorated with flowers. They walked down the wooden dock to a two-person gondola where a gondolier stood in a costume of a black-and-white-striped shirt and black pants with a red sash.

*"Signora."* He reached for Shari's hand to help her into the gondola. Shari sat down on the cushioned red seat and leaned back against the decorative pillows. She took in the traditional decor of the gondola with its flat bottom, Italian throw rug and pointed decorative nose.

*"Signore?"* The gondolier helped Grant in the gondola and he scooted in beside Shari on the seat.

"You like it?" he asked, giving her hand a squeeze.

"I *love* it." Shari certainly hadn't expected Grant to come up with something so romantic.

"Your craft, a *Sandolo,* was imported all the way from Venezia," the gondolier said with a thick Italian accent. "This evening I will take you on a sunset tour of Naples Island through the canals for your recreational pleasure. In the basket you will find chilled champagne and a variety of meats and cheeses."

Shari turned to Grant. "This is wonderful and incredibly romantic."

"Anything for my wife." Grant leaned in closer to Shari and brushed his lips across hers.

The gondolier didn't seem to mind their outward display of affection. Heck, he was probably used to it. He pushed away from the marina with a large wooden oar without saying a word. He took them on a ride through the inland waterways, and serenaded them in Italian. During the course of the ride, Grant popped open the bottle of champagne and poured Shari a glass.

"To us." He held up his champagne flute.

"To us." Shari tapped her flute against his and then took a sip. Then she leaned back into Grant's arms to admire her surroundings.

Their tour took them through several canals, allowing Shari and Grant to see all the decorated homes along the canals. Some were contemporary; others looked like a throwback to days gone by. Many of the homes had their own personal dock with a sailboat or small yacht moored there.

"Look at that." Grant pointed to the sun setting in the distance with various shades of orange, red and yellow. "Isn't it beautiful?"

"Yes, it is." Shari snuggled closer into his chest. She could smell the musky scent of his cologne. It suited him and smelled completely male.

Grant's hand threaded through her hair and he pulled her closer so his mouth could claim hers. And he didn't just claim her mouth; he made her totally his with tantalizing deep strokes of his tongue that Shari returned with a hunger of her own. He kissed her lingeringly, succulently. He tasted her as if he'd never kissed her before. When he finally pulled away, Shari could see lust lurking in his green eyes. "We'll finish this later."

"Promise?"

"I will have you screaming out my name," Grant murmured in her ear.

Once back at the dock, Shari and Grant thanked the gondolier, who received a very generous tip from Grant. Soon they were back in the rental car and on their way back to Los Angeles.

Grant didn't notice Shari was quiet on the ride back because he was lost in his own thoughts. Their day together had shown him what it would be like to really be invested in his marriage to Shari. He had such a pent-up longing for this woman since their college days and now that he'd indulged it, the experience was better than he could have ever imagined. He'd wasted years not knowing what it would be like to kiss her, to taste her, to drive deep inside her until he reached her very soul.

He was falling for her. He'd probably been in love with her from the day he'd met her, but they'd both been too scared to act on their feelings. He'd been waiting for a sign from Shari back then and the only one she'd given him had been the night they'd created Andre. Afterward, he would have given anything for her to say that she wanted to be with him, but she'd shunned him instead by telling him that what they'd shared had been nothing more than a hookup.

That night hadn't been how he'd envisioned being with Shari the first time. He'd wanted to romance her, court her and then make sweet love to her. So his pride had been admittedly stung by her rejection of him.

But Shari wasn't rejecting him now. She was giving herself to him. Last night, she'd been a giving and expressive lover, intent on pleasing him. And she had done that and more. She'd touched him. She'd shown him that they fit together perfectly in and out of bed. Now he just needed Shari to say that she felt the same.

## Chapter 12

When they arrived back at the hotel, the Drayson family was milling around in the lobby, talking and having drinks. Shari didn't see Andre, so she assumed he was upstairs with her mother.

"Look at the lovebirds!" her sister Monica teased, sipping on a green cocktail. Even though Monica was legal, Shari still wasn't used to her little sister drinking alcoholic beverages.

"Hello, hello." Shari waved at everyone. "Did Lillian's bring home another win?"

"We killed it, of course," Drake replied as if her question was ludicrous. "We are the best in the business. Now it's just down to us and Dina."

"Yeah," Monica said. "And I helped."

Shari raised a brow. "Did you?" She thought her sister was more interested in the business side of running the bakery rather than actually getting her hands dirty.

"What country did you get?" Shari inquired.

"Germany," Malik said as he came forward into the middle of the group with her cousin Belinda. Shari could see a touch of lipstick on his lips, which meant they'd been in a corner canoodling. Their wedding was this summer and knowing her cousin Belinda, a perfectionist, everything would be of the highest standard. Thank God she hadn't scared off Malik with her strong and independent streak. He was a great guy.

"That should have been easy," Shari responded. She was familiar with her cakes. "Did you guys do a streusel, a coffee cake or Black Forest?"

Before Malik could answer, Drake replied, "That would have been too easy and that's what Delovely Cakemakers and Brown Sugar did. And Delovely got axed. But me? I'd already done my research online, since Germany was an obvious choice, so we did a buttercream, dark chocolate *Prinzregententorte*."

Shari had no idea what the cake was, but she could see Drake was very impressed with his internet skills. But after her amazing day with Grant, she wasn't about to let anything or anyone get to her. "Good for you."

"Well, we had to rise to the occasion to fight off Dina and Brown Sugar Bakery since you abandoned us in favor of gallivanting with your husband," Drake said. "But no matter. You'll be up against Dina tomorrow."

Shari didn't appreciate Drake's remark. "Gallivanting? We are newly married and we chose to forego our honeymoon to come here."

"Perhaps you should have postponed this quickie wedding until after the competition," Drake returned. "What's more important to you?"

"How dare you question my commitment to Lillian's," Shari shot back, putting her hands on her hips. She could see that several hotel patrons were looking at them, but she didn't care.

"I don't think that's what Drake meant," Belinda said, defending her brother.

"That's exactly what he meant," Shari replied curtly, glaring at Drake. "I've be working there just a tad longer than you, Drake."

"By what, a year?" Drake chuckled. "Look at what Carter, Malik and I are doing with our blog and cookbook. The buzz we are bringing to Lillian's. What are you doing?"

Grant jumped into the fray. "She's bringing Robinson Restaurants, one of the premier restaurant chains, to you. Selling exclusive Lillian's desserts."

"I appreciate you stepping in," Shari whispered in his ear, "but I don't need you to fight my battles." She turned back to her cousin Drake. "I work just as hard as you, Drake, actually longer, because while you're fiddling around on your computer, I'm putting time in the kitchen. Without us worker bees, putting out quality Lillian's bakery products day in and day out, your blog and cookbook wouldn't be a success. Now if you'll excuse me, my husband and I are going to finish our evening."

Shari stalked off toward the elevator, leaving a surprised Grant to follow behind her.

Grant saw the stunned look on Shari's cousins' faces. They probably weren't used to Shari standing up for herself, but she had, and Grant was proud of her.

He found her pacing at the elevator. "Please don't let them ruin our day," he said, taking both of her hands in his. When she didn't look at him, Grant gave them a gentle squeeze.

Shari finally looked up at him and he could see that although she'd put on a good front, tears were shimmering in her eyes. "C'mon." He wrapped his arms around her and led her into the elevator.

Once they were in their room and he'd checked in with Mrs. Drayson and found that Andre was sleeping comfortably in their room, he joined Shari in the living area. "So how about some dinner?"

"I'm not really up for someplace fancy," Shari said.

"That's okay. We can have dinner here at the hotel. They have a highly regarded restaurant with a beautiful view of the Hollywood Hills."

"That sounds perfect."

After a quick shower, Shari and Grant dined in the hotel restaurant. The maître d' set them by the window with a gorgeous view of the city of Los Angeles.

"I'm sorry about earlier." Shari was embarrassed by her family's antics and her reaction to them. She was undervalued by several members of the Drayson family, but tonight was the first time she hadn't taken it lying down.

"Why are you apologizing?" Grant asked. "You didn't start it. Drake was razzing you from the moment we said hello."

"I know, but I shouldn't let it get to me. I'm sure he would be only too happy to tell Grandma that Shari can't handle herself."

"Miss Lillian would be a lucky woman to have you looking after the business because you will love and cherish it as you've done our son all these years."

Shari stared back at Grant in surprise. "Thank you. That's nice to hear."

"I'm not saying it to appease you, Shari," Grant replied. "I'm saying it because it's true. You were right when you said he was a loved and well-adjusted boy."

"It wasn't easy," Shari said. She'd been scared early on when she'd learned she was pregnant and realized she was going to have to parent all by herself. And even though she'd been wrong and Grant would have stepped up, it didn't change the fact that she had been a single mother for four years. "I had to put Andre first and myself last."

"That's what I'm talking about—your selflessness," Grant said. "Not many people have that quality, Shari."

Shari's mouth curved into a smile. "You know exactly what to say to get me out of my funk."

Grant laughed, and the sound of his laughter caused warmth to spread throughout Shari's body. "Good. Because we were having a great day before Drake stuck his foot in his mouth."

Shari nodded in agreement. "We did do a lot. That tour at Warner Bros was great. But the gondola ride, that was the perfect end to the day."

"You think that's the end?" Grant said, leaning back in his chair to regard her thoughtfully. "That was only the tip of the iceberg. You remember what I said I would do to you in the gondola."

Excitement lurched within Shari at the prospect. "I do."

"Then hold on tight," Grant said, "because it's going to be a long night."

Shari could barely remember what she ate even though the food was beautifully presented. The seared scallops with vanilla *gastrique,* zucchini pancakes and wilted spinach were to die for. But Shari's throat had been dry and parched just thinking about Grant's words, so she'd drunk several glasses of the restaurant's best Cabernet Sauvignon. She was just a tad bit tipsy when she and Grant walked back into their suite.

She was unprepared for the sight that awaited her. Their master suite had been transformed into a lover's paradise, complete with lit candles everywhere and rose petals strewn across the bed and floor.

"Grant." Shari turned to face him and was greeted with Grant grasping her face with both hands. He didn't take her lips. Instead, he gently eased into the kiss, licking her lips with his tongue first. Only when she parted her lips, did his tongue dart inside and move in circles, first clockwise, then counterclockwise. Dear God, would she ever tire of his erotic kisses?

When Grant pulled away, Shari felt bereft. "What's wrong?" she asked, looking up at him.

"Nothing, but I have something for you." He grabbed her hand and led her to the master suite where a bubble bath had been prepared in the oversize Jacuzzi tub.

"When did you have time…?" she started, but then she remembered his trip to the restroom at the restaurant earlier that evening. *Sneaky devil.*

"For you, my dear," Grant said. He helped ease Shari out of her clothes, but this time instead of lust and hunger in his ministrations, there was just compassion and caring.

When she was naked, Shari slid her body into the warm, sudsy water.

"Doesn't that feel good after a long day?" Grant asked, sitting on the edge of the tub.

"Oh, yes," Shari said, closing her eyes and leaning her head back on the bath pillow that Grant had placed for her use.

Grant came behind her, rolled up his sleeves and began kneading her shoulders with gentle pressure, releasing any soreness out of her tense muscles. An unconscious groan slid out of her mouth at his long strokes down her back, neck and shoulders. And if that wasn't enough, he surprised her when he grabbed one leg out of the water and massaged her thighs, then her calves and then her feet, wiggling one toe at a time.

The more and more time Shari spent with her husband, the more she realized how thoughtful and romantic Grant could be. Sure, they weren't on an official honeymoon, but Shari suspected Grant would always be like this.

"You relax for a bit," he said. "I'll be back for you."

Grant came back for Shari a half an hour later wearing nothing but a smile. His erection was jutting out and he watched her swallow hard.

He toweled Shari dry and then led her to the master bed. Sitting her on the edge, Grant sank to his haunches. He pushed her thighs open and without saying a word, leaned forward and pressed his mouth against her. Shari writhed in pleasure as he gnawed, licked and ate at her softness. Her inner muscles clenched quickly and she went pliant in his arms, but Grant wasn't done with her yet.

He rolled Shari backward onto the bed, nudged her legs apart and penetrated her hot, slick sheath. He pulled her wrists to her side, pinning her in place so he could thrust slow, then quick, slow, then quick. Shari arched toward him, undulating against him, greedy for more, but Grant was determined to make the night last. His pace was deliberate and steady as he buried himself deep inside her.

Shari's flesh opened to him and the need to possess her, to make her his in every way, was so primal, so carnal that it startled him with its ferocity. But not Shari, it seemed. She met each visceral stroke by thrusting her hips upward.

"You like that?" he asked, circling his hips.

"Grant…oh, yes….yes….yes." Incoherent sounds erupted from Shari.

His mouth wandered back to Shari's and his hands ventured everywhere to stroke her breasts, the curve of her hips and her inner thighs. She felt so slippery, so sweet that the control he had quickly evaporated. Before he knew what was happening, their limbs were tangled in a slow revolution across the bed and Shari was on top, rubbing and sliding over him and then straddling his hips.

She took him on an incremental climb that had him lacing his fingers with hers and straining for release. She quickened the pace and soon they were both crying out as a strong climax took them down in the undertow. And soon Grant's head was lulled against Shari's shoulder as he drifted off into a peaceful sleep.

The next morning, the final day of the competition, Shari awoke ready for battle. The last week had certainly taken its toll on her physically as well emotionally. She'd had ten-hour days shooting *You Take the Cake* and when she wasn't at the studio, she'd been playing tourist with Grant and Andre or making love to

Grant all night. Add Dina to the mix and it had been an emotionally taxing week. She was ready for the competition to be over. Win or lose.

As much as she wanted to curl up with Grant after he'd driven her to the strongest climax she'd ever had in her life, she couldn't bask in it. She rose to shower, leaving Grant asleep in the bed. He wasn't far from her mind, though, as she used the loofah sponge to cleanse her body. Last night, he'd explored her body like he'd found a rare artifact and she'd turned into a quivering mass of limbs and moans.

Turning off the taps, she exited the shower, dried herself and got dressed. As was her style, she pulled her hair back into a ponytail, slid on a T-shirt and skimmed her Levi's up over her hips. She was moisturizing her face when she turned to find Grant naked in the doorway.

Grant rubbed at his eyes. "Why didn't you wake me? I would have showered with you."

"Sorry, babe. I'm trying to get my mind right for the last day of filming today. It's down to Lillian's and Brown Sugar Bakery."

Grant knew what Shari wasn't saying. It wasn't just bakery against bakery. It was personal. It was Shari against Dina. "I understand."

"And as much as I would love to linger in bed with you—" she glanced down and noticed he was happy to see her "—I need to talk to the family. They've all gathered downstairs for breakfast and a last-minute pow-wow. We're pretty sure we'll get the U.S. today as our country."

"I have no doubt Lillian's will be victorious," Grant

said. He saw fire and determination in Shari's eyes this morning. Hell, last night. She was going out fighting.

"What about you?" Shari asked.

"I was thinking Andre and I could have lunch with my parents," Grant shared. "If you recall, they mentioned extending their stay here until we leave."

"Oh, yes, I remember. That sounds like fun."

Grant came forward and wrapped his arms around Shari's waist. "Good luck, Shari. I know you'll do great." He pressed his lips against hers and gave her a searing kiss.

Shari smiled at him when he came up for air. "From your lips to God's ears."

Shari was one of the first Draysons downstairs at the café, ready to discuss last-minute strategies. Drake and Carter joined her seconds later. Drake didn't speak, but Carter came over to her chair.

"Good morning, cuz. How'd you sleep? You ready for battle today?" Carter asked, giving her a kiss on the cheek.

"Absolutely!" Shari said with conviction. "I'm ready to snuff out Brown Sugar Bakery once and for all."

"Sounds personal," Carter said.

Shari looked Carter dead in the eye. "It is. And not just for me, but for Grandma, too. Dina used us. She snaked her way into this family and our business only to start another bakery with some of our recipes, although they've been *tweaked*—" she used her hands to make quotation marks "—to say they were hers."

Carter regarded her. "I like your fire. It's long overdue. And it's a good thing, too."

"Why do you say that?"

"Because the show smells blood. They've been asking about you and Grant. And how Dina fits into the equation."

"Did anyone say anything?" Shari's eyes widened in horror. She didn't want her personal business on display for the world to see.

Carter shook his head. "No, we've all kept mum."

They didn't finish their conversation because Monica, Belinda and Malik, her parents and Grandma Lillian and Grandpa Henry soon joined them. "Is everyone ready to go win this competition?" Grandma asked when she arrived.

"Yes," they all said in union.

"Then let's go get that trophy," Grandma Lillian yelled.

At the studio, tension was thick in the air. On one side, Dina and the Brown Sugar Bakery team, on the other, the entire Drayson clan. Shari, Carter and Belinda were in the final round while the rest of the family sat in the audience. All of them together were an intimidating sight, and Shari hoped Dina was quaking in her boots for a Drayson family smackdown.

"Are the teams ready?" Brandon, the host asked.

"We are." Shari, Belinda and Carter had already donned their aprons and were standing by their table in the studio.

"So are we," Dina and her team yelled from across the room, not to be outdone.

"The final country in the cakes around the world week is…" Brandon paused for effect, looking at both teams. "You guessed it! The good ole United States."

Everyone clapped in the studio. "As you know, we're

taping live today to see which of these two teams will stand victorious in the end." The host faced the camera. "Will it be the underdog and one-woman show at Brown Sugar Bakery, Dina English? Or will it be a Chicago staple and institution, Lillian's bakery?" More cheers erupted. "Let's find out on the final round in 'Cakes around on the World' on *You Take the Cake!*"

Shari stared across the room at Dina when they went to commercial break. The time had come for the final battle. Who was the better baker? Shari or Dina? Her eyes connected with Dina's from across the room and Shari saw the fierce look in her former friend's eyes. Dina was out for blood, but this time so was Shari. She leaned over and whispered in Carter's ear. "Let me take the lead in this battle."

"Shari, you know I'm the master cake maker," Carter whispered hotly.

"This isn't about you being the best," Shari responded. "I *need* to do this."

"What are you two whispering about?" Belinda asked, joining their conversation.

"Shari wants to take the lead," Carter replied, looking nervously at Belinda, then Shari again. He'd assumed, given his reputation and that he was the oldest, that he would naturally run lead as he'd done the other two rounds when they'd worked together.

"For Christ's sake, just let her!" Belinda shrugged, looking across the room at Dina and her team. "We don't need this derisiveness right now."

"Fine!" Carter huffed.

As the show came back from commercial break, Shari silently whispered a thank-you to Carter, but he gave her only a curt nod.

"As in the previous battles, you will be judged on taste, creativity and presentation," Brandon said. "We'd like you to come up with three miniature cakes reminiscent of the South. To find out your mystery ingredients, open your boxes."

Shari rushed to open the box first and found sweet potatoes, popcorn and orange soda. "Are you kidding me?" she said aloud.

Carter looked inside the box. "You wanted to run lead, so what you got?" He raised an eyebrow.

Shari's mind began frantically racing. And then she said, "Carter, I want you to make a sweet-potato cake with that famous honey-maple glaze of yours. Belinda, how about a twist on an orange-soda pound cake? I'll leave you to the ingredients. And I'm going to make a triple-chocolate cake with candied popcorn."

"Like Cracker Jack?" Belinda asked.

Shari nodded.

Carter smiled at Shari's plan, but didn't say a word. Instead, he, along with Belinda and Shari, went racing around the kitchen pantry and refrigerator to collect their ingredients and start making their cakes. During the first round, Shari came around to Carter's bowl to taste his sweet-potato batter.

"Delicious as always," Shari commented.

"As if you expected anything less," Carter teased and bumped Shari with her hip as she went back to her area. "Listen, I'm sorry about before. I know how much this means to you."

Shari smiled in return. "Thank you, and I won't let the team down."

She returned to her station to finish pouring her chocoholic batter concoction into miniature pans and then place them into the convection oven to bake. When they were in the oven, she went to the stove to check on her oil for her popcorn. Once it was popped, she poured the popcorn into another pot with a candy thermometer where she'd been heating sugar to turn to syrup along with some peanuts. She stirred the mixture until it was gooey and then transferred it to parchment paper to cool.

"Looking good, kid," Belinda said from behind her.

"Thanks. I think so, too."

And she was right. Her triple-chocolate cake with candied popcorn was a hit with the judges. And for the first time, she beat Carter in praise from all the judges.

"Great round," Carter said when time was called for a break before the second challenge.

Shari tried not to let the praise go to her head, but it was the first time she'd beat Carter. Dina was next to go down. She was determined to crush Dina and show her that you couldn't mess with a Drayson.

"So, you and Shari," Grant's father said after lunch later that afternoon. "I didn't see that coming." They'd decided to take an afternoon stroll along the boardwalk and Andre and his grandmother had walked ahead of them while Grant and his father hung back to talk.

"How would you?" Grant asked. He hadn't kept in touch with them in years other than a quick trip at the holidays.

"Touché," his father responded. "I guess I haven't really been a part of your life these last few years, not since your divorce from that Dina woman."

"That marriage was a mistake."

His father regarded him curiously. "It was just as quick as this one. What's the difference?"

Grant stopped in his tracks and turned to glare at his father. "The difference is that it's Shari I've always wanted."

Warren Robinson's brows slanted into a frown. "Then why did you marry Dina?"

"If you recall, you impressed upon me that I needed to settle down and…well, Shari rejected me back then and I guess my ego was somewhat bruised."

"And Dina was all too willing to put some salve on it?"

Grant cocked his head to the side and looked at his father. "Something like that."

"And now? Shari clearly hasn't rejected you. She married you."

"Only after I found out about Andre."

"And did a little arm twisting, too?" Grant's father knew him well, because in some ways Grant was a chip off the old block.

"I wanted Andre to have a two-parent household," Grant said firmly.

"Yeah, well, that isn't always for the best."

"Are you talking about you and Mom?" Grant queried, thawing his tone.

"Your mother and I have made our peace with our circumstances. She likes the life I provide and the status that comes with it."

"And you? Are you happy, Dad?"

His father shrugged dismissively. "I'd resigned myself years ago to the fact that Eleanor was no longer the woman I married. That she was cold and distant. And then, when she met Andre, I saw a whole new side of her. For the first time in years, I've seen a glimmer of the woman I hadn't seen in a long time, especially once she started drinking."

"Hold on to that side, Dad," Grant said. "Don't let her go. And for God's sake, get her into AA."

"I've tried," his father said, taking a seat when they stopped walking, "but your mother adamantly refused. And after we lost touch with you, well…it became worse. Perhaps now that she has something to live for, a reason to want to get sober, she'll reconsider."

"I hope so," Grant replied, "because if she doesn't, she won't be a part of Andre's life. I won't have him grow up watching his grandmother get drunk." When he'd returned home during college, the mother he'd once known, who was always home after school, who came to every sporting event and cooked a slew of food when his friends came over, was gone. She'd been replaced by a sullen and withdrawn woman. Often, he would walk in during the middle of the day to find her three sheets to the wind.

"I completely understand." His father nodded in agreement. "You're very protective of Andre."

"I have a lot of time to make up for. And not just to him, to Shari. I feel like we wasted so much time apart when we could have been a family from the start."

"Don't beat yourself up too much, son," his father said. "You're doing all you can now. Have you told Shari how you feel?"

Grant looked at him in confusion. "What do you mean?"

"Have you told her that you're in love with her?"

*Love.* The four-letter word he'd been avoiding saying out loud. He hadn't really ever said it to anyone, not even to Dina. The word scared him. He was more a man of action and showing Shari how he felt about her rather than tell her. Although he knew she was independent, he wanted her to know that he would take care of her always. "No, I haven't."

"Why the heck not? What are you waiting for?" his father inquired. "People need to hear you say you love them. Maybe if I had said it more to your mother, she wouldn't be in the place she's in now. And if I'd said it to you, you wouldn't have felt the need to disappear out of our lives."

Regret resonated in his father's voice and caused tears to form in Grant's eyes. "Say it now, Dad."

"I love you, Grant. I always have and I always will. You're my boy." With one arm, he reached over and pulled Grant into a hug.

Grant couldn't remember the last time his father had hugged him, but he was glad he had now. If a man as proud as his father could admit he'd made mistakes, maybe it was time Grant did the same. It was time to tell Shari that she was the love of his life. That all the women before her had merely been placeholders for her. And there was no better time than the present. The last face-off with Dina was sure to cause Shari anxiety, and whether Lillian's won or lost, knowing that Grant was beside her, loved her, would be the icing on the cake for Shari.

Grant rose to his feet. "Dad, I have to go. Would you and Mom be willing to watch Andre? You can meet Shari and me back at the hotel." Grant checked his watch. "Say 8:00 p.m.? It's a long day of filming."

"You would leave him with us?" his father asked, surprised by his son's faith in him.

Grant nodded. "I trust you. And I have someplace I need to be and that's with the woman I love." There, he'd said the words.

"Go get her, son."

## Chapter 13

Shari was nervous. The judges had been divided on Round 2 on who'd made the best cake featuring Iron Man for the third movie's premiere. All three judges had been complimentary about Lillian's Iron Man cake creation in which they'd had to use crispy rice bars for the bulk and height of the superhero and air brushing to get the desired color, but they had eventually chosen Brown Sugar Bakery as the final winner. The judges felt Brown Sugar Bakery did a slightly better job. Shari tried not to let it get her down and reminded herself that it wouldn't be much of a show if Lillian's swept all of the challenges. Of course they had to let Dina win. Or at least that's what she told herself.

Since the country was the United States, in the third and final challenge, the show tasked the bakers with paying homage to men and women in uniform by making a custom cake and display that represented America for a military gala later that day.

"Since we're asking you to create a masterpiece in four hours," the host said, "we'll give you a craftsman to help with the display and some helpers in the kitchen." He pointed to six women standing nearby on the set.

Shari looked at Drake, Malik and Monica sitting in the audience and blurted out, "I don't need any helpers. I have my family. Can they assist us?"

The host raised a brow and looked at the producers. They'd clearly never had a contestant try to change the rules. The producer was shrugging his shoulders, so the host turned to Dina. "Does Brown Sugar Bakery have a problem with Lillian's using their own bakers?"

"Perhaps they think they need the help," Dina said pointedly, looking directly at Shari. "I'm confident that I'll be fine with your bakers. Why don't you come over?" She motioned the women over to her table.

"Well, then." The host turned to Shari's family sitting in the audience. "Drayson family, c'mon up."

Drake, Malik and Monica eagerly left their seats in the audience to come on the set and don aprons.

"Great idea!" Drake whispered to Shari. "Call in reinforcements when you need help."

Shari was surprised by Drake's off-handed compliment. She didn't know if he meant she couldn't handle the task or that he was happy to be included, but she chose the latter. "Thanks. Now huddle up, team." She motioned her family forward.

The producer seemed to love the Drayson family camaraderie and had several cameras focused solely on them. Shari noticed Dina glaring at her and shrugged her shoulders before returning to the group.

It was a daunting task, but together, the Drayson clan came up with a display that would incorporate the five arms of the military, and the cake would be decorated in red, blue and white fondant and vanilla buttercream. They would top the cake with American flags, stars, dog tags and medals made of fondant. Doing each fondant piece individually would be time consuming, but Shari was sure the cake and display would be a winner.

Malik, Carter and Drake would focus on crafting the delicate pieces of fondant into works of art while Shari, Belinda and Monica would make the cake batter for the enormous four-foot tiered cake.

They barely had time to finish the batter before the host was calling a break. The Drayson team left the set for a fifteen-minute break.

"So how do you think you're doing?" Grandma Lillian asked when they came to the audience seating area. She looked at Shari since she was running lead.

"Good, good," Shari said confidently. "It'll be tough, but we'll do it. Won't we?" She looked at her cousins for affirmation.

"Yes, you will," Grant said from behind her grandmother.

Shari's heart turned over in her chest. What was he doing here without Andre?

Grant saw the concerned look on Shari's face. "Don't worry. Andre's with my parents. I thought you could use some moral support."

Her mouth spread into a wide grin. "Thank you. It's a dead heat right now, but I'm positive Lillian's will take it home."

"Glad to hear it. Well, I'll just be here in the background if you need me," Grant said, joining her parents.

The buzzer sounded, signaling the end of the break and they returned to the set. Over the next hour, Shari and her family worked as a unit, prepping and putting the cakes in the convection oven. When the next break was called, Shari was happy with their progress. That's until she saw Dina leaving the set and walking over to Grant in the audience.

All color drained from Shari's face. What was Dina up to now? She was finally in a good place with Grant and didn't want any drama.

The producer watched Shari on set and walked over to the director. "The action is happening off set." He inclined his head to Dina who was walking up the stairs toward Grant. "And look at the wife." He glanced at Shari, staring daggers at Dina from across the room. "Get it all on film."

"Are you sure this is the direction you want to go? It's invasion of the contestants' privacy," the director pleaded. "They didn't sign up to have their personal life on television. They signed up for a baking competition."

The producer waved him off. "Just do as I say, okay?"

Grant sighed when he saw Dina climbing the steps. He was not ready for another go-round with his ex-wife. He wanted to keep the peace today for Shari's sake.

"May I have a word?" Dina asked.

Grant looked at the stage and saw how upset Shari was. This was bad timing. Shari needed to be focused on the competition not on his conversation with Dina. "Now is not a good time."

"This won't take long."

"Fine." Grant sighed. He wasn't oblivious to the

curious stares Shari's family was giving him as he walked down the steps and away from the set. He did notice however that a cameraman was holding a camera nearby, but why would they film him? He wasn't even part of the competition, so Grant ignored him.

"Before I leave here today I just want to reiterate to you that I had no idea Shari was pregnant when we graduated. If you believe nothing else, believe that," Dina said.

"You don't have to explain anything at this point, Dina."

"I know, but I just need you to know that I'm not the kind of person to keep a parent from their child." Dina spoke with quiet, but desperate, firmness.

"You're just the type to keep your best friend from the man she wanted," Shari said from behind her.

Dina spun around and rolled her eyes upward. "Not this again. Listen, Shari. It's not my fault you had a cheap one-night stand with Grant and you weren't woman enough to step up to him at the time. But you need to stop blaming me for your troubles. I repeat, I did not know you were pregnant."

"Cheap?" Shari said, her voice becoming louder. "Maybe you should look in the mirror. You were the one that went after my leftovers."

"Ladies, ladies." Grant tried to step in between the two women, but Dina pushed him out of the way and stepped directly in front of Shari.

"Your leftovers?" Dina laughed shrilly, throwing her head back. "You didn't even know what to do with Grant. I'm the one that became his wife first. You're never going to be anything other than second best!"

"You witch!" Shari lurched after Dina, but Grant

grabbed her by the waist with her legs kicking and flailing to prevent her from attacking Dina.

"Back at you!" Dina continued her rant. "If Grant hadn't found out about Andre you'd be a dried-up spinster. Why? Because you've always been your family's walk-off mat. You've been so busy trying to fit into their image of how you should be, you don't even know yourself."

The entire Drayson family had rushed out of their seats when Dina went after Shari. They came to stand behind her now in a united front against Dina.

"We got your back." Shari was surprised to hear Drake whisper.

Tears started rolling down Shari's cheeks. Dina's words were cutting her like a knife. But this time she fought back, wiping away her tears. "You were the one who was nothing more than an orphan in college."

Dina cringed at Shari's words as if she'd been physically punched, and clutched her stomach.

"*My* family took you in. We treated you as part of our family. *I* brought you into Lillian's. Without us and the training we gave, where would you be? But instead of showing us some appreciation, you bit off the hand that fed you. And you think you're better than me? I don't think so. Look who I've got!" Shari motioned to her family behind her. "I've got my family and the man I love." Then she noticed that the camera was rolling and that *You Take the Cake* had been filming their entire interlude.

Dear Lord, what had she done? Had she really just told the world and Grant that she loved him?

Dina broke into tears. "You're right. You have *everything,* Shari. You have a family who loves you, a career that's in your blood and thanks to the Drayson family wealth, more money that you know what do with. You've never had to worry a day in your life."

"And you were jealous of me, weren't you?" Shari asked. "So you lied to Grant about me and Thomas so you could have him for yourself. For once in your life, admit the truth, Dina."

"Fine. I was jealous," Dina admitted with a stiff upper lip. "And when I saw you and Grant together, it was one more thing that you had that I didn't. The one thing I could count on was being popular and beautiful and sexy."

"You had something else, Dina," Shari said, coming forward. "You had me."

"And now I don't," Dina replied bitterly, stepping backward. "And now you've taken something from me this time. You have my ex-husband. Does that make you feel good, Shari?"

Shari stared at Dina and saw the hatred, the jealously, the contempt in her eyes and couldn't take it a second longer. Pushing past her family, she dashed out of the studio. A cameraman was on her heels, but she outran him and rushed out the building.

Grant had been silent while the women hashed out their past, but he was not going to stand idly by a second longer. "This is not a game, Dina. I am not some prize to be won."

"I...I didn't mean it like that," Dina began, but Grant cut her off.

"I will not let you cause my wife another minute of pain. I love her, Dina. I always have. It was always Shari." And with that comment, he raced after Shari.

When a cameraman tried to follow Grant, he turned on his heel and warned, "You follow me and you'll regret it."

The cameraman held up his hands in defeat and slowly began backing away.

Grant found Shari outside across from the studio warehouse, pacing the pavement. "Can I talk to you?"

"I just humiliated myself in front of millions of people and put all of our business out there for the entire world to hear." Shari sniffed, pointing to the building. "You must be sorry you ever met me."

"I'm only sorry that Dina and I hurt you so much back then." He rushed toward her and gently wiped the tears from her face with the pads of his thumbs. "I had no idea back then how you felt about me."

"It's not your fault," Shari said, shaking her head. "I didn't speak up. I just let Dina sink her claws into you and then when I found out I was pregnant, I didn't tell you the truth. That's on me."

"We can't rewrite the past," Grant said. His eyes brimmed with tenderness. "What's done is done. All we can do now is start fresh."

"Really?" Shari asked, blinking back tears. "You mean you don't want to divorce me for humiliating you?"

"Quite the opposite," Grant said, bending down on one knee in the middle of the studio lot. "I'd like you to marry me."

Shari looked confused. "We're already married."

"I know, but I want to do it right this time. I want to recommit myself to you."

"You do?"

"Yes." Grant smiled up at Shari. Her eyes were glistening with tears, but she'd stopped crying. He was happy because he was finally going to say what had been in his heart for some time. And now that he knew Shari felt the same, he was ready to shout it from the rooftops. "I love you, Shari. From the moment we met in college, I thought you were something special, but you didn't seem to notice. I thought you weren't interested in me. We traveled in different circles back then. But then that night, when we made love, I thought okay, she *is* interested. She wants me, too. But then you told me our night together didn't mean anything and it broke my heart. And if truth be told, my pride was wounded."

"I had no idea."

"How could you? Because I stupidly started dating Dina. She pursued me and I let her. It was a mistake marrying her. One that I will regret until the day I die. And then a few months ago, I heard about this rising baker in Chicago named Carter Drayson and I decided to come see for myself if you were still as smart and beautiful as I remembered. Imagine my surprise when I found out about Andre. I was so angry with you for keeping the truth from me that I couldn't see straight."

"Is that why you browbeat me into marrying you?"

Grant colored. "I know our marriage didn't start out on the right foot. But the last few weeks have reminded me that the feelings I once had are not only still there, but have grown stronger. The bottom line, Shari, is that I love you and I can't imagine my life without you."

Finally. He'd told her how he felt, and now he saw tears fill Shari's brown eyes. "I want to have a real marriage," Grant continued. "I want to share my bed and my life with you. I want more babies with you. And if you'll have me, I'll spend the rest of my days proving to you that you are not second best or runner-up. You and Andre come first with me, always."

Shari clutched her chest. "Oh, Grant, I love you, too!" She threw herself into his arms and started planting kisses all over his face. "And I'll happily marry you again and reconfirm our vows because I am hopelessly, desperately in love with you."

"Oh, Shari." Grant went to kiss her again, but Shari held her index finger to his lips.

"I am so sorry I kept Andre from you, but I'm so thankful that you can forgive me and we can start over. I want to have a dozen of your babies."

"Well, a dozen is kind of a lot," Grant said, laughing as he held Shari in his arms.

"Okay, well, maybe not a dozen. All you need to know is that I want to spend the rest of my life with you."

"But first you have to get back inside and finish that show," Grant said. His face turned serious. "Your Grandma, hell, your entire family is counting on you."

Shari shook her head. "I don't know if I can go back in there, Grant. I humiliated myself in front of my family, in front of the world. And Dina. All those awful things we said to each other. We can't take those statements back."

"No, you can't." Grant nodded in agreement. "But Dina can't hurt you or us anymore. She has no more power over us. We've made our peace with the past and are about to start a new chapter of our lives together. You go in there and knock 'em dead. And I promise you, babe, I will be here cheering you on."

Shari smiled. "Okay, okay." She reached for his hand and together they walked back into the studio.

* * *

Once inside the studio, the cameraman was right there again, nipping at Shari's heels. "Mrs. Robinson," the producer said approaching behind the camera, "you do realize we're in the middle of a live show here."

"I realize that," Shari returned. "But you do realize that I am here to represent Lillian's Bakery in a bake-off, not so my personal life can be fodder for your show." Shari winked at Grant and then walked back onto the studio floor.

Her family instantly swarmed her inside the studio and started with a barrage of questions. "Are you okay?" "What happened earlier?" "Is there anything we can do?"

Shari was surprised they weren't berating her for walking off during the middle of the competition. But it certainly wasn't her fault that the slimy producer was trying to use her relationships to gain better ratings. She raised her hands. "I'm fine. I'm fine. Grant and I talked." She turned to her husband at her side. "Had a long talk and everything is great. Better than that, actually." She beamed up at her husband. "So...I guess the question is...is this competition still going on?"

"They went to a commercial break, which included a long spot by one of the sponsors of the show, but we're due up in minutes," Belinda replied.

Her father came toward her and grasped both her hands in his large calloused ones. "If you're still up to it, baby girl."

"Your father is right," Grandma Lillian said. "I had no idea that the bad blood between you and Dina went so deep. If I had known, I would never have put us in this competition."

"Grandma, this isn't your fault," Shari responded to her grandmother's obvious guilt at the turn of events. "A lot had gone unsaid between me, Dina and Grant all these years. There was lot of hurt, anger and betrayal. And it wasn't solved today, but at least it's off my chest."

The host, Brandon, came toward the Drayson family. "I'm sorry, but we can't stall any longer. If Lillian's intends to continue with the competition and not forfeit the win to Brown Sugar Bakery, we need you back on set."

"We're not forfeiting," Shari said defiantly. "We're in this to win it. C'mon, troops." She started toward the stage, but noticed her family didn't budge.

"Are you sure about this, Shari?" Carter inquired. "Because as much as we want to win this, we don't want to cause you any more pain."

"And you're not. I'm not a victim. I'm capable of taking care of myself. Now, let's go." She urged Carter, Belinda, Drake, Monica and Malik forward. "The clock is ticking."

## Chapter 14

Seconds later, they were back on set. Shari glanced across the kitchen set at Dina. Their eyes connected for the merest of seconds. Shari didn't see the animosity she'd previously seen, but she did see Dina's fighting spirit. She wasn't going down without a fight, but that was okay with Shari because she was ready to give her one.

The cakes that they'd taken out of the oven before the previous break had cooled sufficiently in the freezer thanks to the nearly half hour it had taken for them to reconvene. Shari, Belinda and Monica went about frosting the cakes and getting them ready for Carter's bedazzled American flags, stars, dog tags and medals made of fondant and covered with sparkly dust.

"Thirty minutes," Brandon called out.

"C'mon, guys," Shari said as they started covering

the cakes with the fondant, "we've got to move it. We're running out of time."

The Drayson grandchildren and Malik worked together tiering the cakes up to their four-foot height and decorating each layer. The craftsman had done a wonderful job of creating the display that would house their work of art. The four-tiered display jutted out in four directions and housed a giant aircraft, submarine and tank to show the different branches of the military. Red, white and blue were prominent colors in the display, but not too overwhelming.

Shari glanced over at Brown Sugar Bakery. They, too, had done a great job of incorporating the American military theme with large soldiers of the different branches on their display. She couldn't tell what kind of cake Dina had made, but she was sure it would be a showstopper.

"Five minutes," Brandon called out.

Shari hustled around the display, making sure every piece was centered and every decoration was executed perfectly.

"Looks good, doesn't it?" she said, standing back for a second to admire what they'd created.

"It looks great, sis," Monica replied. "Despite all the drama, you really came through."

"Thanks, kid." Shari gave her a quick squeeze and then leaned over to fix a fondant piece on the display that had come loose. "Perfect!"

"Time!" Brandon yelled out. "Contestants, step away from your displays."

Belinda, Carter, Drake and Malik joined Shari and Monica near the center of the kitchen where Dina and her team had also assembled.

The host walked over to the contestants. "After a week of competition, after numerous rounds of showing your versatility in a bake-off around the world, it comes down to one final evaluation from the judges. Which bakery can deliver the entire package of taste, presentation and creativity in an amazing display? We'll find out after the break."

The cameras stopped rolling.

"Wow! That was intense." Malik was the first one to speak.

"That was more than intense," Shari replied. "I don't think I have a name for it."

"I do. It's sadistic torture that producers use on contestants," Carter replied. "See just how much we can throw at a bakery before they crack. I mean really, a week's worth of competition? Usually the show is one episode."

"Well, they did say they wanted the best of the best," Belinda added. "And they were looking to see what bakery would crack under the pressure."

"And I nearly did," Shari said. "Crack under pressure, that is."

"But you came through in the end and that's all that matters," Drake said, coming over to her and grabbing her shoulders in a firm squeeze. "You're made of tough Drayson stock."

"Why, Drake, is that a compliment?" Shari asked with a hint of sarcasm.

Drake frowned. "I know I don't give them to you that often, Shari, but you know I love you, right?"

"Hmm…" Shari paused as if she didn't know the answer. When Drake guffawed, she finally responded. "I do, but it's nice to hear it once in a while."

"Well, I do," Drake replied. "Love you, that is. And no matter what happens today, you were a great leader."

Shari smiled. "Thank you."

"We're back in one minute," the director stated.

Shari looked up to find Grant in the audience holding up a sign that read GO SHARI. Where in the heck had he gotten that poster? She didn't have time to ponder because the cameras began rolling again and the director was putting his hands up with the countdown.

The host, Brandon, walked over to Brown Sugar Bakery's team first and asked, "So how do you think you did?"

"I think we did a great job," Dina said. "I had a hard-working team here." She high-fived the two members of her staff and the *You Take the Cake* helpers. "We created a masterpiece. I think Lillian's will find this isn't a slam dunk after all and that they've got some serious competition for the crown as *You Take the Cake* champion."

Brandon came over to the Lillian's Bakery team. He walked over to Shari first. "Shari, you took the lead today in the competition. Any particular reason?"

Shari gave an honest answer. "I'm not an over-the-top person. What you see is what you get. I wanted to show that sometimes the person you underestimate can be the same person to wow the socks off you. I wanted to be that person today."

"Do you think you were successful?" he inquired.

"I know so," Shari said, confidently facing the camera. "I had the entire Drayson family with me." She walked toward her cousins and Malik. "The most skilled bakers, right here in the trenches with me. We created a signature work of art that you would be hard-pressed to duplicate."

"Well, you've heard it, folks," Brandon said as he turned back to the camera. "Both bakers think they have the winning recipe. Let's hear from the judges."

The camera followed Brandon to the judges' table, and the director came forward to both teams advising them to relax in the green room while the judges deliberated.

As Shari was leaving the set, the producer walked toward her. "Mrs. Robinson, about earlier…"

Shari put her hand up to his face. "Save it for someone who wants to hear it," she said and sashayed toward her family in the audience.

"Pick up your jaw," Carter said, laughing at the director. "You wouldn't want any flies to get in."

"You guys were wonderful!" Grandma Lillian said when the rest of the family joined the Drayson contestants in the green room. "Win or lose, I couldn't have been prouder of you."

"Don't count us out, Grandma," Shari said. "We haven't had the last word yet." When she saw Grant behind her, she jumped in his arms and pulled his mouth to hers.

Belinda smiled at the newlyweds' display of affection. "Shari's right. Did you see what we accomplished?" She pointed to the towering American cake they'd created. "No matter what Dina did, she can't top that."

"That's my baby," Malik said, throwing his arms around Belinda and embracing her.

"Oh, Christ, not you, too," Drake said. Shari could

tell he'd had about all the lovey-dovey he could take on this trip. He was a bachelor for life and didn't want or need a significant other.

"Don't knock it," Carter said, laughing from his side. "If Lorraine was here, I'd be doing the exact same thing."

Grant pulled Shari away from her family to a private corner of the studio. "You did a phenomenal job out there," he gushed. "I'm so proud of you, Shari."

"Thanks, honey." She beamed from ear to ear. "I don't know if it was clearing the air with Dina and getting everything I'd held in all these years off my chest or whether it was the fact that we declared our love for each other, but whatever it was, I felt such clarity out there on stage, a sense of purpose, a sense of fulfillment that I haven't felt…well, since Andre was born."

"What was that like?" Grant asked. They'd never discussed how things had been for Shari when she had Andre.

"Childbirth?" Shari chuckled, glancing at her husband. "I don't think you want to know about the fourteen hours of labor your son put me through."

"No, no." Grant shook his head. He didn't need to know the gory details. "What was it like holding our son in your arms for the first time? What was it like knowing you'd brought a new life into the world?"

Tears filled Shari's eyes. "It was marvelous," she replied. "It was the most amazing feeling I've ever had in my life. And overwhelming."

"How so?"

"Well, seeing him for the first time I was filled with such joy. I didn't know it was possible to love another human being as much as I loved Andre and at that same time feel fiercely protective of him. But there was also fear. Knowing I was responsible for this little life—" Shari held both her hands together in a bowl shape "—who fit in my hands. I didn't know how I was going to take care of him, being a single mother and all, but I did."

"You never have to worry about that ever again," Grant said fiercely, "because I will play a major role in our children's lives from the time of conception until they're old and gray."

Shari leaned over and kissed him. "And I wouldn't have it any other way."

"Ladies and gentlemen," Brandon said as he faced the audience and the cameras, "after much deliberation, the judges have reached a decision. Contestants, can you come forward, please."

Dina and her team and Shari and the Drayson family walked to the middle of the set.

"After a long, hard battle, there's one team whose display the judges feel is a step above the other and whose cake the judges couldn't resist. And the winner is…Lillian's Bakery!"

Balloons and confetti streamed down from the ceiling at the announcement. Brandon walked over to Shari. "As the winner of *You Take the Cake*'s Cake Around the World week, Lillian's Bakery wins $100,000." The host handed her a large cardboard check in that amount.

"Thank you, thank you." Shari was ecstatic and smiling from ear to ear. She'd delivered. She'd carried her team, her family to victory. The entire Drayson family came forward to help hold up the cardboard check as the cameras faded to black.

Monica, Carter, Belinda, Malik and Drake all leaned in for a big group hug to celebrate their win and although Shari was on cloud nine, she looked over at Dina from across the room. She looked defeated and alone as she packed up her belongings with her team.

Slowly, Shari disengaged herself from the group and walked over to Dina.

Dina looked surprised to see her. "Come to gloat?" she inquired.

"Quite the opposite." Shari held out her hand. "I came to say, good fight. You had us against the ropes."

Dina looked at Shari's hand for several moments and Shari thought she wasn't going to accept her gesture, but then Dina shook her hand. "But you guys won fair and square. Your cake was better. Perhaps I should have stayed at Lillian's longer and perfected my technique."

Shari frowned.

"I meant it as joke," Dina said with derisive laugh. "I appreciate you coming over here, especially after today's catfight."

Shari shrugged. "Let today be the end of all the bitterness and anger, Dina. Let's agree that we all—you, me and Grant—made mistakes in the past. Let's make a clean break."

Dina paused as if thinking about Shari's request. "I think you're right. It's time to let go of the past and let bygones be bygones. I wish you and Grant lots of happiness."

"I wish you the same," Shari said and turned and

walked away. She was excited for what lay ahead with Grant, but somewhere in the far corners of heart, she was sorry to say goodbye to someone she'd once called a friend.

# Chapter 15

"We're late." Shari shifted uncomfortably in her seat as they drove up to the Drayson estate in Glenville Heights for a family dinner. The entire family had returned from the trip to Los Angeles almost two weeks ago, but Shari and Grant had stayed longer because Grant had surprised her with a honeymoon to Hawaii. They'd been on the island of Maui for well over a week and had just returned the previous day and found out they'd been summoned.

"Didn't you say you're always late thanks to our son back there?" Grant asked from the driver's seat.

"I know," she said, "but today is different. I think Grandma Lillian is going to announce who's going to take over Lillian's Bakery."

"You really think so? I mean, it's so soon after the competition."

"She has to be," Shari responded. "Why else would she make it mandatory that all family members attend the dinner?"

Grant shrugged. "I guess we'll find out soon enough."

Fifteen minutes later, Grant's Mercedes Benz pulled into the estate, but they had to park farther down the drive, thanks to the number of cars already present.

"Looks like everyone's already here," Shari said as he pulled Andre from the car seat.

"Don't worry so much," Grant replied as he grabbed the bottle of wine he'd brought as an accompaniment for dinner.

When they opened the door, the party was already in full swing. Monica opened the door. "We were wondering where you guys were," she commented.

"Thanks to this one—" Grant pointed to Andre who was sitting on top of his shoulder "—we had a slight delay."

"Blame it on my nephew." Monica laughed. "C'mon in."

She led them to the living room where the family had assembled. Her grandmother and grandfather were in their favorite spot, their love seat big enough for two. Her parents, Dwight and Lisa, were seated on a sofa, where Monica joined them. Her aunt Daisy and uncle Matt were adjacent on another sofa. Drake, Belinda and Malik were all standing nearby, while her uncle Devon and Carter and his fiancée, Lorraine, were standing near the fireplace.

Shari and Grant joined her parents by the couch. Shari bent down and brushed a kiss across her mother's cheek and squeezed her father's shoulder. He smiled up at her and Grant and reached for Andre on Grant's shoulders. Andre settled into his grandparent's lap and Shari sat on the arm of the sofa. Being the first Drayson great-grandchild, he was spoiled rotten, Shari knew, but once Belinda and Malik or Carter and Lorraine started a family, he was going to have to share his grandparents' attention. But that was just fine with her, because Shari knew that she and Grant would provide Andre with all the love and attention he would ever need.

Lillian watched her children and grandchildren. She'd waited a long time for this moment. She was about to speak and tell them why she'd gathered them all to her home, when her son Devon spoke.

"All right, Mother, everyone's here now," Devon said, his arms folded across his chest. "Spill the beans."

"Don't rush me, Devon," Lillian admonished. "I will talk in my own time."

"I'm with my brother on this one, Mom," Dwight said. "You gathered us all here for a reason and we are all eager to hear what you have to say."

"Well, first I'd like to propose a toast." She motioned for the servers who'd been standing at the back of the room with champagne flutes to come forward.

"First, I want to commend all of my grandchildren and Malik on an outstanding job on the show." Grandmother Lillian looked around the team that had taken the bakery to victory. "You showed what hard work and determination can bring—success. Join me in a toast to winning *You Take the Cake!*" She held up her flute and the family joined in a big toast and clicked glasses with one another.

Once the ruckus died down, Lillian rose from her

love seat. "I'm sure you all wondered why I entered the bakery into the competition."

"It did come to my mind," Drake replied honestly. "I mean, reality television isn't your style, Grandma. It's more my speed."

"True." Grandma nodded in agreement. "The reason I signed the family up was because of all the bickering going on at the bakery. Who's better than whom. Who's in charge of whom. I wanted it to stop. I wanted you to see that family is more important than anything else."

Lillian noticed several family members mumbled underneath their breath, but they were wise enough not to speak while she had the floor.

"And I achieved my goal," Lillian continued. "You finally stopped fighting long enough to understand the meaning of family. The way you all worked together as a team day after day to beat your competitors was a sight to behold. But more important, the way you stood behind Shari when she and Dina battled their past demons filled my heart with such joy." She clutched her chest.

"Oh, Grandma, we're sorry to have ever caused you any grief," Belinda said, rushing to her side at hearing the tears in Lillian's voice and grabbed her hands.

"I know you are, sweetheart," Lillian said, patting Belinda's hand. "Which is why your Grandpa Henry and I can leave knowing you all will work together as a team. I think the competition showed you each your strengths and weakness and what you excel at."

"You're leaving, Ma?" Daisy asked. "When? Why?"

"We'd like to see the world," her husband, Henry, answered instead. "We've seen enough of Chicago. We want to live a little."

"That's right," Lillian added. "We'll be gone for about six months." When the murmurs subsided, she said, "I know it seems like a long time, but I also know I'm leaving the bakery in good hands."

"But to whom?" everyone asked almost in unison.

"You see, I knew you would all be wanting to know who I selected," Lillian replied, "And it's all of you."

"I don't understand, Ma," Dwight said.

"I was never going to choose one child over another." She looked at Dwight and Devon and then at her only daughter, Daisy. "I was never going to choose one grandchild over another." She looked at Carter first because she'd always known that he'd felt less a Drayson even though she'd tried her best to treat him equally. Then she glanced around the room at her other grandchildren—Drake, her spitting image Belinda, Monica and then her shyest grandchild of all, Shari.

She'd seen the toll that the competition and Shari's reunion with Dina had taken on her granddaughter, but Shari had stepped up to be the woman Lillian knew she could be. The once shy and most unassuming grandchild of all had finally blossomed. She supposed it was because she'd finally married her one true love, Grant Robinson, with whom she shared a child.

"There is a wealth of great talent in this room because you are all great bakers. Some of you went to college for an education and can run the business side of the corporation and Lillian's, including our family holdings in real estate. So instead of bickering about who's over whom, why don't you excel in what you do best." She walked over to her eldest son Dwight and lightly stroked his cheek. "You are my firstborn and naturally Lillian's is yours as first in line, but you are already running the corporation and I think you should continue to do that as CEO."

"And you, baby girl." She went to her daughter Daisy, who was sitting with her husband, Matt. "You have always been good with numbers. Dwight will need a hand with the corporation's books, and no one knows money better than you. I think CFO is a fitting title for you, my darling."

Daisy nodded at her mother. "I couldn't agree more. Thank you for your faith in me."

She walked over to her youngest son, Devon, who was already starting to pace the floor. "Continue to run my real-estate holdings. You love the wheeling and dealing and are better at it than anyone I know."

Then she walked over to Drake. "You love to bake, but it's your secondary passion. You're the king of social media and this publishing opportunity you have with Malik and Carter is your calling. So pursue it on behalf of Lillian's. I know you will make it a great success."

Drake agreed. "Well, you know, ever since the show aired, our website, Facebook and Twitter pages have been blowing up. Many have asked if we'd consider opening a store in Los Angeles. I think with the combination of winning the show and our cookbook, we could take Lillian's nationwide. And I'd be willing to take the helm."

"Exactly." Grandma Lillian walked over to Belinda and Malik. "Drake is on to something, but he needs help. I think you two are amazing bakers and you two could be the right combination to help open a bakery in Los Angeles."

"You really think so, Grandma?" Belinda asked, looking somewhat surprised by the turn of events.

"I sure do." She smiled broadly and then turned her attention on her eldest granddaughter, Shari. "And you, you showed such promise in Los Angeles when you led us to victory, which is why I think you should run the front of the house at Lillian's." Shocked murmurs escaped the group, but Lillian continued, "With your business acumen like your idea for cake mixes, you'll keep Lillian's on course and help bring us into other fine-dining restaurants like your husband's Robinson Restaurants." She gave Grant a friendly wink.

"What about me, Grandma?" Monica piped up.

"Your sister," Lillian looked to Shari, "will need some help running Lillian's. You've been great at following her lead with the cake mixes. Learn from her. It will only help you grow as a businesswoman."

"I will, Grandma," Monica said, glancing at Shari sitting on the opposite end of the couch and giving her a smile. "I promise."

Lillian knew her family had all figured out that if Shari was going to run the business aspect of Lillian's that left only one person as executive baker.

She watched Carter's eyes grow wide from across the room. "That leaves you, my dear boy." Lillian slowly made her way over to the mantel where he stood speechless with Lorraine by his side.

"You've come into your own all these years and I think you're the fitting choice for executive baker at Lillian's." Carter opened his mouth to speak but Lillian cut him off. "And that's not to say that Carter runs all of you," she said, facing the group, "only that his experience and reputation have *earned* him the right to lead in the kitchen. That being said, I am giving each of you equal shares in Lillian's, which means equal voting power. Come together as a family as you did to win *You Take the Cake* and we'll be stronger than ever."

After the initial shock of the evening had worn off and the family was still mingling throughout the house, Grant pulled Shari away and into a nook in the hallway.

"How do you feel?" he asked. "About your Grandma's decision."

Shari laughed. "The truth of the matter is she really didn't say anything that we didn't already know. She just shone a light on our talents. Perhaps the only surprise was her request that Drake, Belinda and Malik might want to consider opening up another bakery in Los Angeles."

"I guess so, because your family took it all in stride. There were no raised voices or screaming matches."

"Well, Grandma kind of laid down the law," Shari said, laughing. "And I think we all respect her enough to abide by her wishes."

"So with Carter leading the kitchen does that mean I will have you all to myself longer during the mornings?" Grant inquired.

Shari raised a brow. "Why? Did you have something in mind?"

"Hmm…well, actually I do," he said, swiftly pulling her into a nearby room and planting the most delicious kiss on her lips. A kiss that reminded Shari that although circumstances had kept them apart for years, they were destined to be together.

# Epilogue

*Three months later*

"**Y**ou sure your family won't mind that we're using the kitchen?" Grant inquired as he took in the smell of baked goods wafting throughout Lillian's kitchen. He eyed several custom cakes that were sitting in the see-through refrigerator awaiting delivery. He turned back to watch Shari baking.

"Why would they?" Shari inquired, smiling at her husband. "We're making cupcakes for Andre's softball team."

She'd never felt such happiness and contentment in her entire life. She loved Grant and he loved her. Every day he made sure she knew just how important she and Andre were to him. He'd shown her by relocating the corporate office for Robinson Restaurants to Chicago to ensure his time away from them was minimal because that's the type of husband and father Grant wanted to be.

They'd been in the kitchen for hours making chocolate and vanilla cupcakes for nearly twenty five-year-olds. Shari had used the industrial-size mixer to make various frostings from chocolate to strawberry to peanut butter ganache that she was sure the children would love.

Andre and Grant were in the kitchen "helping" her, although Shari could hardly tell from the mess the two of them had made eating all the cake batter out of the bowl.

Shari smiled when she looked at Andre. His mouth and face were covered in cake batter. She continued adding sprinkles, M&M's and sparkle dust to the various cupcakes. She knew how much kids liked color.

"Can I help, Mommy?" Andre asked.

"Of course you can, sweetheart." Shari pushed the container of sprinkles in his direction and allowed him to decorate the cupcakes. More of the sprinkles ended up on the counter than on the cupcakes but Shari didn't mind. Andre was such a precious gift to her and now that Grant was a part of their life, she'd watched him blossom. Her life was so rich, she couldn't ask for anything more.

"Look, Mommy! Look what else you made!" Andre startled Shari out of her daydream.

When Shari looked up again, she saw Grant holding a baby in his arms. Surprised, she walked over to see for herself and when she peered down into the baby's eyes she saw the cutest little girl with green eyes and a slightly dimpled cheek.

*Ring. Ring.* Shari awakened from sleep with a start

at the sound of the alarm. What a crazy dream! Or was it? Shari tried to remember the date of her last period, but couldn't. She'd missed it!

She turned over to find Grant sleeping peacefully beside her. She shook him gently and he sleepily rolled over to face her. "Honey, I think I have something to tell you…"

\* \* \* \* \*

**New York Times Bestselling Author**

# BRENDA JACKSON

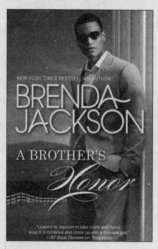

The *Granger brothers left behind their family's Virginia estate—and the bad memories it holds—years ago. But their dying grandfather's request to make things right has brought them home…*

As the eldest brother, attorney Jace Granger is determined to take responsibility for his family's failing business. As CEO, he hires a consultant to turn the company around. Smart, sexy Shana Bradford is the right person for the job—and the right woman to turn Jace's world upside down.

But old secrets begin to emerge. A woman from Jace's past suddenly reappears. And an explosive discovery changes everything Jace thinks he knows about his mother—and his father, who was convicted of her murder.

Jace soon learns he needs to face the past…or risk losing his future.

### Available wherever books are sold.

**Be sure to connect with us at:**

Harlequin.com/Newsletters

Facebook.com/HarlequinBooks

Twitter.com/HarlequinBooks

HARLEQUIN® MIRA®
www.Harlequin.com

MBJ1433

# REQUEST YOUR FREE BOOKS!

## 2 FREE NOVELS
## PLUS 2 FREE GIFTS!

KIMANI™
ROMANCE

### Love's ultimate destination!